# COWBOY SEEKS A ROMANTIC

EAGLE MOUNTAIN BROTHERS, BOOK 2

MARLEY MICHAELS

# 1

## MOLLY

S omething is up. I don't know what. I don't know *why* I'm feeling this way. But it's like I've got a sixth sense that something in the universe isn't quite right tonight. I have to ignore it though because the Lion's Lair tavern is pumping for a Tuesday and I'm dishing out drinks and handing out meals like there's no tomorrow. There's country music blasting over the speakers, competing with the loud thrum of conversation as local ranchers and townsfolk talk and yell, and wind down after a long day. The energy in the bar is at an all-time high. Yet despite that, I feel like the walking dead.

Maybe it's just because I'm so goddamn tired it's a miracle I'm still standing. But surviving in a perpetual state of exhaustion isn't new to me, working three jobs and raising my three siblings to keep my family together, all done with a big—

albeit, sometimes fake—smile on my face, is my new normal. Or it *has* been recently, anyway.

A quick glance at the clock reminds me I still have three hours of my shift left, which means at least three and a *half* hours until I can collapse face-first into bed for a maximum of six hours before I've gotta get up, shake myself off, and do it all over again tomorrow. *The life of a responsible adult who just happens to be a surrogate parent to three.*

But I could be a zombie and I'd still feel the presence of Beau Barnes in the same room as me. Ever since he walked in with his brothers, Jesse, Randy, and Sawyer and Kendra—Jesse's wife, my boss at the Vet Clinic AKA job number one, and my best friend—I've found my gaze drifting over to their corner, smiling to myself, and sometimes not even realizing I'm doing it. Something about that man just makes me feel...calmer.

Eric, my boss here at the Lair—job number two —keeps me on task though, making sure I've always got something to do. Once this happy hour crowd dies down, it should just be the regulars and the old-timers who don't wanna go home alone. *Then* I'll have a small chance for a breather.

I like working at the tavern; it fills my adult socialization quota every night I'm here. I get good conversation, a few laughs, and great tips. All of which go into my birthday and Christmas fund for the kids and pays for their extracurriculars. Because when you've suffered the loss of not one but *two* parents, you hang out for the good times to drown out the sad ones. So I do everything I can to make sure those good times are *amazing* ones.

When our father passed away suddenly a few years ago, I vowed to my two brothers and sister that our little family would be my sole focus. I'd live, die, and bleed for them just to keep us all together. I gave up college where I was studying to be a nurse and dedicated my life to raising my siblings. That's why I work as hard as I do, why I made that decision to give up my life and aspirations to make sure Colson, Sage, and Cody have the best possible life they can have and get all the chances in life to do whatever they set their mind to. It's a small sacrifice to pay for their eternal happiness.

My third job—yes, *three*—is being an errand girl around my small hometown of Kinleyville for anyone who needs something done for them. That ranges from grocery shopping, baking, dog walking, helping Ellie-Mae out at the Barnes family's supply store, and even filling in when Beatrice is short of workers at Betty's Diner. You name it, if it helps them out and they're willing to *pay* me for it, I'll do it. Sometimes I don't even get paid in money. My old high school English teacher, Mrs. Murphy, gives me a never-ending supply of freshly laid eggs from her chicken coop and surplus fruit from her backyard orchard. Or there's even Mr. Morrison down at the boat shop who'll give me a fresh fish or two for dinner. All of it is appreciated, even if I am more than aware that I'm the town's resident charity case. Beggars can't be choosers and three kids are *not* cheap to clothe and feed when you don't have a college degree or any trade skills to lean on.

But at the end of every day, when I get home, I know I've worked hard for everything we have because I refuse to take handouts, and I flat out deny anyone who wants to give us charity without my offering of something in return. That's my own stubborn pride though. Call it my fatal flaw, because I will happily die on that hill.

Unfortunately, my work and family obligations leave very little time left for me. I haven't had a date in...I can't even remember how long. Unless, of course, I count the night I got the job here at the tavern while out boot scootin with Kendra, Jesse, and the very gentle and kind, Beau.

I sigh whenever I think about him. If I was older, less responsible, and didn't have the world balanced so precariously on my shoulders, he's definitely the kind of man I'd want to date—probably the *only* one. He's the perfect romantic hero rolled up in a handsome rancher package that any woman within the town limits would want to unwrap. But he's out of my league due to all of the above, and even if he *was*, I think the fact that I'm close to half his age would be enough to put a pin in that idea.

"Molls, you OK?" Kendra says, appearing out of nowhere opposite me. I lift my head and meet her furrowed gaze. "You look like you need a break."

I lean my elbows onto the counter and throw her a sardonic smile. "Is that your polite way of telling me I look like poop?"

She reaches over and rests her hand on my arm. "It's me checking on my person to make sure she's not burning her seemingly never-ending candle at both ends."

Shooting her a grin, I shake my head. "I'm OK, Kendie. I'm just—"

"Worn out? Drained? Struggling to be everything for everyone?"

A snort escapes my lips, chased by a resigned sigh. "I'd just kill for a gallon of strong coffee and twelve hours of sleep."

"You should get the recipe for Ellie-Mae's cowboy brew. That will give you a caffeine kick for days and have you bouncing on air," Kendra's husband, Jesse, says, coming up behind my best friend and wrapping his arms around her.

Kendra grins up at him, her eyes going all soft and gooey, serving as an unfortunate reminder of everything I want but can't have right now—that being a *life*.

And as they've done most of the night—hell, every night I'm working and Beau Barnes is at the Lair—my gaze drifts over to where he's standing, beer bottle in hand, watching the dancefloor and laughing with his brothers, Randy and Sawyer.

*Snap out of it, Molly.*

I could if he wasn't so damn dreamy.

To look at, Beau's quiet and strong with an *amazing* smile, dark blond hair that's a little long on top, the perfect length to run your hands through. Then his gentle giant brown eyes are so deep and rich in color that it makes you wanna dive into them and never come up for air. Plus, there's his big bulky, *tattooed* body that is the epitome of a man who works hard on the land and has the muscles to show for it. All of that would be enough to make any girl melt like a popsicle on a hot day. But then there's his personality—something only those of us lucky enough to spend a little one-on-one time with him get to recognize. He's attentive, doesn't miss a thing, and loyal as the day is long. He's also sweet, kind, and has a dry wit that he only lets fly when he's comfortable or knows you well. I see him as one of those silent alpha types that waits and watches until it's time to *take* what he wants.

I may be romanticizing the guy because I know it'll never happen between us, but those silent alphas are a favorite of mine in romance novels I read. They're protectors, nurturers, men who want to take all your troubles away and carry the load while encouraging their heroine to be the best she can possibly be. The quiet alpha is the stuff dreams are made of, and I like to look at Beau and imagine *all* of those things. I'm like a little girl crushing on her dad's best friend or something. I probably seem pathetic, but it's all the action I have in my life right now.

"You know," Jesse starts, his eyes going to the corner where his brothers are gathered before returning to me. He wraps his arm around Kendra's shoulders as he rests an elbow on the bar. "My brother probably needs another beer. Maybe you could go deliver it to him?"

Kendra bites her lip, my eyes crinkling at the sides. "I think he might be *real* thirsty."

Jesse grins down at her. "*Parched*, even."

I fix my narrowed gaze on the two lovebirds. Ever since they came here months ago for their first date and dragged me and Beau along, they've been trying to play matchmaker and get me and Beau together.

Except I made my thoughts on *that* particular scenario very clear to Kendra, and probably Beau too when he called me a few times after our double date and I got so caught up in life stuff that I didn't get back to him. We're on friendly terms though. So there's that at least...

And really, it's better this way. Friendship is all I can offer these days, and let's just pretend a man like Beau—who, like his brothers, has all the women in town vying for the chance to set their cowgirl boots next to his bed at night—could even *be* interested in me. I think he deserves something more than *just friends*. Add to that our age gap and the fact I can't have a life until my youngest brother, Cody, is of age, then I have even less to give. So romantic thoughts aside, the only focus I can have right now is working and navigating life's ups and downs. Then when Cody goes off to college, I'll start living again. That's the plan, anyway.

Pity that by then, I'll be thirty and Beau Barnes will be forty-five and most likely married with a gaggle of mini-ranchers running around. I'll have missed my chance by a long shot. So it's best to not even entertain the *possibility* of Beau and me...

*Fake it till you make it, Molly.*

I straighten and make quick work of getting another round of drinks for Jesse and his brothers, adding the beers to his tab and getting him to sign off on it. He thanks me, then Kendra and I watch him take them over—my best friend doing so with a swoony 'girl in love' expression on her face.

"He's right, you know," she says.

"About what?"

Kendra arches a brow and commences a staredown with me, one which I win because, *hello*, I live with two teenagers. She acquiesces with a sigh. "Oh, all right. I'll let it go." *That* makes me smile. "I'll try to say goodbye before we leave for the night."

"Look forward to it, Kendie. And thank you."

Her head jerks. "For what?"

"For being my person and standing by me even when I *know* you don't agree with some of the decisions I make."

"Babe, you are the most selfless, hard-working, determined, and dedicated woman, sister, and *person* I've ever met. I'm honored to be your best friend and have your back, whether you need it or not." I have to blink rapidly to stop my eyes from stinging. "*But...*" she says, waving her hand in the air in front of me. "This whole 'work yourself into the ground and sacrifice everything for everyone else' gig is going to break you if you're not careful."

"I—"

She levels me with a stare. "All I'm saying is keep an open mind, OK? Don't shut yourself off to something just because you *think* you have to dedicate everything you have to everyone else. We're allowed to be selfish now and then. It's human nature. Actually, it's a human *need* occasionally. So..." she says, shutting me up when I open my mouth to argue. "I'll leave you be for now. But know that we all want what's best for you. Yeah?"

"Thanks, babe."

"Right. Now, Neville Nightingale is at the end of the bar drooling over that bottle of Jack on the shelf, so I think you might wanna go put him and his liver out of their misery."

I giggle and glance down the bar. And sure enough, one of the regulars is eying up the liquor bottle like he's a starving man in a desert and that's his oasis.

"See you at work tomorrow?" I ask her as I slowly move away.

"Sure thing. I'll be there with bells on."

"Forget the bells. But I won't say no to Betty's Bear Claws."

"Done deal," she says with a laugh, lifting her hand in a salute before moving through the crowd, leaving me walking down the line to serve drinks and do what I seem to do best these days —work my butt off.

An hour later, I walk out from the kitchen with a tray of freshly washed glasses, sliding them onto the bar and grabbing a cloth to polish them ready for tomorrow. As I do, my eyes scan the room, surprised and disappointed when I see that Kendra, Jesse, and the Barnes brothers must've left while I was out back. It's not even close to last call yet either, so I feel a little bereft knowing they're no longer here, which makes no sense. I've worked many a night here over the past six months where my friends haven't been here eating, drinking, and dancing the night away. But tonight, I've felt... *off*. So maybe they're feeling that shift in the air too?

Something feels different and despite wracking my brain over it while serving drinks and nattering with the bar's regulars all night, I haven't been able to work out *what* or *why* I'm feeling this way.

That's until a knock on the bar pulls me from my thoughts and my eyes lift to the soft, gentle chocolate-brown gaze of Beau Barnes standing not far from me. I shoot him the most camouflaged smile I can muster, his brows narrowing to the point of confusion as he looks me up and down, seemingly conflicted by something. "What is it?"

"Molly, we've got a problem." My head jerks, and now I'm the one frowning.

"*We* have a problem?" What kind of problem could Beau and I have at ten on a Tuesday night? He's not making sense.

"The kids are outside in my truck."

Now I'm *really* confused. "What kids?"

"*Your* kids."

"*What?*" I say, dumping the dishcloth I was holding and shucking off my apron while hurrying around the end of the bar. As a thousand scenarios run through my head, my chest gets so tight I can barely breathe and my heart feels like it's stuck in my throat choking me. *Why are the kids out this late, let alone hanging around a bar? Please let them be OK.*

"Just stop for a minute. Take a breath," Beau says, blocking my frantic escape by resting his hands on my shoulders and dipping his head down so that he's all I can see. "It's gonna be OK."

I frown. "What is? They should be at home safe. Not in a car with a strange man."

His brow arches high. "Strange man?"

"Ugh. You know what I mean."

"Yeah. Well, *this* strange man picked them up hitchhikin' about three miles back. Seems your car had a mishap."

My entire body goes still, my blood running cold.

"*What*?"

Beau looks over his shoulder. "Eric. Molly's got family business. She's clocking off for the night."

"All good. I'll cash out your tips tomorrow, Molls." I hear his words, but I'm too far gone to let them register as Beau reaches down and takes my hand, my heart thundering as he leads me out of the bar. I'm so discombobulated, it's like my mind and my body aren't even connected anymore. All I can hear is my breath and the thump, thump, thumping of my pulse in my ears, and all I can think about is the kids *hitchhiking*, a car *mishap*, and god knows what else life is about to throw at me.

I should've paid more attention to my gut feelings instead of trying to ignore them, because all night

I've felt off, and now it's obviously time to pay the piper. The universe was obviously trying to tell me something, and now I guess I'm about to find out exactly what that was.

## 2

## BEAU

"What were you thinking?" Molly hisses through gritted teeth at her brother, Colson, while he stands against the side of my truck looking sheepishly at his feet.

"Don't know," he mumbles.

"Don't know isn't an answer, Cols."

He looks up at Molly and frowns, and I can see the war going on inside his mind—does he argue? Or just tell the truth and accept the punishment?

Hanging back, I try to avert my eyes so as not to embarrass the kid. I feel for him. I really do. From what I know, he's a generally good kid. I never hear of him getting into any trouble around town, which shows how well he's been raised considering he's a seventeen-year-old almost man who's practically as responsible for his two younger siblings as Molly. Hell, considering his circumstances—the loss of their mother when Cody was born, and the loss of their father three years ago —I'm surprised he isn't in constant trouble. A kid dealing with loss, tied to home with little to no social life is an explosion waiting to happen. When I lost my father, I was a grown man, and it was hard enough to cope with. Losing the man I'd looked up to my entire life, someone who helped mold the man I'd become, left a fairly big void in my chest. I imagine Colson feels something similar too. So I don't envy this kid at all. I don't envy any of them. But I sure would like to make things easier on them, which isn't easy when Molly is so incredibly proud and determined to do things without any help.

"We wanted ice cream," Colson mutters finally, gesturing to fifteen-year-old, Sage, and eleven-year-old, Cody, who are both sitting in the backseat of my truck, pretending they aren't hanging on to every word being said. "We weren't doin' any harm."

"You totaled my car."

"It's not totaled. It just broke down."

"Because you wanted to go out for ice cream? There's ice cream in the freezer, Colson. You didn't need to go out at all!"

"God, Molly. We just wanted to *do* something. We're always cooped up in the house while you're at work and we were bored and our friends were at Betty's and—"

"So you totaled my car to hang out with your *friends*?"

"I didn't total it!" he shoots back, his dark eyes flashing. "I didn't even know there was something wrong with it."

"Why do you think I didn't drive it to work tonight?"

"I thought you just caught a ride." He holds his hands out and shrugs.

"And you didn't notice the big red engine light on the dash? It's kind of hard to miss because it beeps too."

"People ignore them all the time, and it stopped after a while. I thought it'd be OK for a short trip, but then everyone wanted to go out to the lake and—"

"You were taking a fifteen-year-old girl and an eleven-year-old boy out to the lake on a *school* night?" Molly releases a sardonic laugh and folds her arms across her chest. "I can't believe you."

"We were only going for a little while. I thought it'd be OK."

"You thought? I think that's the one thing you didn't do, Colson. Because you know damn well that while I'm out here working my butt off to support all of you, the only thing you should be doing is staying home, studying, and watching your brother and sister." Colson opens his mouth to speak, but Molly stops him. "We're trying to make our lives better here, Cols. Not harder. You should've all been in bed by now, not making late night excursions. Where the hell did you even get the money to take them to Betty's, anyway? Because you know how I hate charity."

"I've been walkin' the neighbor's dogs. They pay me for it," he admits, folding his arms to mirror Molly's stance.

"You're working?" Molly pulls her head back and frowns.

"It's just dog walking," he mutters, but she looks hurt. "I do it after school before dinner."

"Three jobs, Cols. I work *three* jobs so you can concentrate on school. If you wanted money, all you had to do was ask. If you want to hang out with your friends. All you have to do is ask me."

"And force you to work even more? We barely see you as it is. I want to help, Molly. Why won't you let me do something more than just babysit? You know Sage is old enough to watch Cody. I could get a job and you wouldn't have to have three. We could share the load."

"No!"

"Why? I want to help!"

"Because you're destined for more than this!" Molly yells, pointing to herself as she does. "You're supposed to have a normal life where you go to college and parties and—"

"I don't even like school!"

Molly gasps. "What exactly are you trying to say here? That after all this work and sacrifice, you don't even want to go to college?"

Colson kicks at the ground and shrugs. "Maybe," he says, lifting his eyes to hers. "I dunno yet."

Molly holds her hands out to the side and looks my way, releasing a huff of air that seems to say that she can't believe what's happening right now. And while I sympathize with her frustration and admire the fact she's been working herself ragged to give her siblings the chance at a college education—something she herself had to give up—I also understand the Colson's frustration. He's on the cusp of adulthood and he's barely even gotten to be a kid. Losing one parent is hard. But losing both feels impossible. And by the sound of it, he's conflicted, torn between making his sister proud and the weight of responsibility that comes with being the man of the house too.

"He doesn't want to go to college," she directs at me, laughing incredulously. "What am I supposed to do with that?"

Taking a deep breath, I offer her an understanding smile before reaching out to open the passenger door of my truck. "You sleep on it," I say, gesturing for her to hop inside. "It's late, it's been a long night, the kids are tired, and you are too. So how about you both take a step back, get some rest, and discuss this with a clear head in the morning?"

"A long night," Molly repeats while Colson takes the opportunity to end the conversation and jump into the back with his siblings. When the door closes, Molly runs a hand through her blonde hair and turns to face me. "It's been a long three years. And it'll be at least six more before anything slows down. I'm exhausted, Beau. And for what? So my kid brother can end up just like me?"

"You're doing an amazing job, Molly. Don't sell yourself short," I say as she presses her mouth into a thin line before sliding into the front seat and closing her eyes.

"Am I really doin' that great, though?" she says when she opens her eyes again. "'Cause from where I'm sittin', this looks a lot like a shit show."

"Just a tiny bump in the road that'll seem even less so after a good night's sleep," I say before she smiles a little, and I shut her in, willing her to understand that everything gets easier in time.

When I round the truck to the driver's side, I catch Colson's eye and he offers a half smile to me in thanks. I mouth to him that it's going to be OK, and he seems assuaged some by that.

On the way from the Lair to Molly's place in the foothills of Eagle Mountain, we don't make a heck of a lot of conversation. Molly seems to be quietly seething in the front seat, while the kids sit in the back, unwilling to say something in case they make the situation worse.

Molly lets out a groan when we pass her truck. It's still smoking slightly, so I'll get a buddy of mine to look at it in the morning and assess how bad it is. But for now, I'm just grateful I saw them walking along the road when I did. Wandering the streets late at night—even in a place as friendly and close-knit as Kinleyville—isn't a good idea at any age, but hitchhiking, now that could get you killed.

"Thank you for doing this," Molly says when I pull into their driveway and the kids jump straight out. "I know I lost my cool back there, but I can't tell you how grateful I am that you found them when you did and that you got us all home safely. It means the world to me, Beau."

"Any time. I'm happy to help, I mean that."

With a smile, she places a hand on my arm and squeezes gently. "You're one of the best men I know. I'll find a way to repay you, I promise."

"No need," I say, feeling my throat thicken at the way all the little hairs on my arms have just stood up in response to her touch. It's like an electrical current has sparked in the air and is prickling against my skin. *What the hell?*

"Well, I want to," she says, hopping out of the truck. "Thanks again."

I nod and wait for her to reach the front door and let her and her siblings inside. But as I watch her enter the house and the lights go on inside, I can't help but place my hand over the space on my arm where hers was. It's still tingling. I've never felt anything like that before.

## 3

## MOLLY

After sleeping in fits and spurts all night, my mind whirling over all the things that could've happened to the kids as they *hitchhiked* to the tavern, I give up trying to rest and I'm already sitting in the kitchen with my second cup of coffee in hand when a bleary-eyed Colson emerges from his room.

Now, in the light of day, I'm torn. Initially, I was livid, and couldn't understand why he would ever think it was a good idea to go out in the truck at night. Then I was worried about all the what-ifs and possibilities of things that could've gone wrong if Beau *hadn't* seen them and pulled over, or if they'd accepted a ride with an out-of-towner with nefarious intentions. Sage is a fifteen-year-old girl for crying out loud, and Cody is not even twelve. Colson is older, yes, but it's not known—and hopefully never will be—whether he could defend himself and our siblings against a grown man or even multiple people. And thinking I'd be OK with them going to the *lake* late at night? Ugh!

Around four a.m, I realized that the person I'm most annoyed at isn't my brother, it's *me*. I'm their legal guardian. I should be here to supervise them. So if anything had—or ever does—happen to them under my watch, it's on me. All me. No one else.

With a healthy dose of caffeine coursing through my veins now, I also see the other side of things. Colson was trying to do something nice for Sage and Cody. It was ice cream and a chance to see their friends. That's it. His intentions weren't bad, he just wanted to give them a treat.

*How can I be mad at him for that?*

"Hey," I say softly. I can hear my dad in my head saying, 'I'm not angry, I'm disappointed,' and it's those words that are on the tip of my tongue. Last night while Beau was dropping us home, I held my tongue, and when we *did* get inside, we all went to bed, Colson being uncharacteristically quiet. Cody was near-on asleep on his feet, and Sage just huffed and disappeared behind her bedroom door.

Colson jerks his chin by way of a response and moves straight for the coffeemaker, pouring himself a hearty mug and barely leaning his hips back on the counter before taking a drink.

I watch him, waiting for his gaze to lift to mine, and when it does, I can see that I'm not the only one struggling this morning.

"Look, I—"

"Cols, I don't—"

We both stop, Colson's lips twitching before he tips his head, urging me to go first.

"Don't worry, I'm not gonna go all—"

"Crazy?"

"You guys are my responsibility."

"Sage and Cody are my responsibility too. I'm the one staying home every night to keep an eye on them and don't get me wrong, I don't mind it. But it was *just* ice cream, Molls. If the car hadn't broken down, we'd have been just fine."

I open my mouth then slam it shut again, the clarity clouded since last night slapping me in the face like a wet salmon jumping out of the water. And dammit, my seventeen-year-old brother *knows* he just got one over on me, especially going by the knowing grin curving his lips.

Taking a deep breath, I sigh and shake my head. "OK, yes. You've got me there. And *Yes*, that *was* a nice thing to do for them." His lips part to talk, but I forge on. "*But*," I start, "you're not eighteen yet. And although nothing *bad* happened to you guys last night, I would still be held responsible if it did. And I'd also never forgive myself if something *had* happened. *That's* why I was so angry. Seeing you guys out there on your own scared me."

Colson's eyes harden. "I would *never* let anything happen to anyone I care about. You, Sage, and Cody are everything to me."

Fuck, shot to the heart right there. I stare into my brother's eyes and it hits me just how much I've underestimated him. He's offered many times to get a job to help us out, and I've flat out refused. That's why I took the job at the Lion's Lair. But in making that decision, I also gave him my trust to look after them. *That's* what he was doing.

And when I'm working, I have to trust that he'll look after things and be 'me' when I can't be here. In my shock and worry about finding out they were not only outside the tavern, but had been found walking along the road in the middle of nowhere. I'd forgotten that.

I get up and walk over to him, reaching out to cup his shoulder, hating his wary expression and tense body language. "I'm sorry, OK. I wasn't here, and I know I should be. But I'd rather work all hours of the day to give you guys everything you need, and—"

"Molly, stop. I get it. Just…" He huffs out a breath and his shoulders finally relax. "Look, I shouldn't have hitchhiked. I should've stayed with the truck and waited for someone to drive past or something. Cody was a bit down after being run out at his baseball game after school and then Sage got a text to say some of our friends were at the diner, so she suggested we go grab an ice cream. We shouldn't have agreed to go to the lake, I get that. But then the truck broke down and…"

"The rest is history, huh?" I offer him a wry smile. "How about we call it a learning experience and move on?"

"Sounds good to me. Just don't feel guilty for not being here, Molls. We all appreciate everything you've done and *are* doing for us, even if it doesn't seem so sometimes. And all I wanna do is help you to do that. If you don't want me workin', then I'm gonna step up and be the responsible *almost*-adult when you aren't here. That's my job as the next oldest, and as the man of the house."

"I'm a man too!" Cody says, appearing out of nowhere in the kitchen doorway.

I shake my head at him. "Squirt, you're an *almost*-teen."

The eleven-year-old grins and bounces a shoulder. "I've got hair on my chest. That makes me a man. Cols said so."

"What?" I screech. *No. Hell no. My baby brother does* not *have hair on his chest.*

"See!" Cody says, lifting his shirt and pointing to his pecs.

We lean in and squint.

"Right there," Cody insists. "See!"

I jerk my eyes to Colson, and we both try not to laugh. There is *zero* hair on that kid's chest. Unless we're counting tiny baby hairs, and everyone has those.

"Dude, put it away. You'll hurt my eyes," Sage says with a laugh, coming up behind Code and wrapping an arm around his neck, pulling him in for a noogie.

"Ugh. Stop!" he whines, tugging down his shirt. "You'll make my hair fall out!"

"What hair?" Sage laughs, and soon we're all chuckling. Then Sage looks over to me and arches a brow.

"You over your freak out about last night?" She walks over to grab a mug and helps herself to a coffee. I used to frown upon her drinking it, but as she, Colson, *and* Kendra have all reminded me, Sage is fifteen, and it's not like she's a four-cup-a-day addict like I am. *Kids, man.*

"Um, *no*. But Cols and I have sorted it out."

"Good. Cause you can't be angry at us. It's not like *we* made the truck overheat and shit a brick."

"Sage, language," I groan.

"What? So Colson can swear like a drunken sailor, but because I'm a *girl*, I'm not even allowed to say 'shit'?"

"Shit's not a bad word, Molls," Cody *helpfully* points out. I swing my entire body around and point my finger in his direction.

"You *definitely* can't say shit. Sage, try *not* to curse in front of your brother."

"Yeah, Molls. Whatever you say, Molls," she says in a flat drawl that just makes the boys grin at her.

"Ugh. You kids are gonna turn me gray by the time I'm twenty-four."

"So not far away then?" Colson teases, earning evil eyes from me.

"Right. Enough. It's not 'pick on Molly day.' Let's start getting ready for school cause you're all gonna have to catch the bus, and that leaves in..." I look at my watch and freak. "Shit, thirty minutes. C'mon, people. Chop chop. I'll make lunches while getting breakfast ready, y'all go get dressed and get your bags packed."

"Aye, aye, captain," Cody says with a snort before spinning on his heels and running back down the hall to his room.

"I hate the bus. How long till the truck is working again?" Sage asks. *Shit.* In all my freaking out and stressing over what happened last night to the kids, I blocked out the fact that now we've got another bill to add to our already tight budget—car repairs.

I groan and scrub my face with my hands. "I'll sort it out. I'll call Rob at the mechanics and see about getting the truck towed there and a quote for the repairs. Maybe he'll let me do a payment plan with him or somethin'."

"Rob's son Paul is on the football team. I can talk to him if ya want." I shake my head, my gaze softening when I meet Colson's serious expression.

"Thanks, but going straight to the person is usually best. It'll be fine. I can always pick up another shift or two at the Lair. Eric's already offered to help me out with overtime if I ever need extra money or—."

"Molly, you work enough as it is."

"It's fine." *Shit, damn, fuck.* It's not, but I'm not going to let the kids know that. I'll protect them from everything I have to keep them cool, calm, and happy. They're kids, that's what kids deserve.

He rolls his eyes. "Just promise me you're not gonna burn out, OK? I meant it when I said you can trust me to look after you all. You've just gotta believe me." My heart aches in my chest at the absolute earnest and determined look on his face.

"You're totally reminding me of Dad, you know that, right?"

This time he smirks. "Good. Now let me go get ready for school. Classes to ace, teachers to charm, girls to—"

I narrow my eyes. "Don't *even* finish that sentence, Colson James Roberts."

All the brat does is wink at me before topping up his cup and disappearing to his room like the other two, leaving me to make a start on breakfast and preparing their lunches before getting them out the door for the bus.

Except we don't even get that far because not ten minutes later, my left hand starts to itch like crazy and that same weird feeling from last night washes over me just as a heavy door slams shut outside.

Curious, I lean forward and peek out the kitchen window just in time to see Rob the mechanic, standing beside his tow truck. *What in the world?*

Quickly wiping my hands, I move to the front door and step outside, stopping dead in my tracks when I see that not only is Rob and his truck parked in my driveway, he's towed my *truck* home too.

"Ah… hey, Rob," I say, totally confused and bewildered.

He looks over his shoulder as he removes the tow hook from the undercarriage before standing up straight and turning to face me.

"Hey there, Molly. Sorry I couldn't get here any earlier, but I did a quick fix-it job to get her runnin' again so you could get the kids off to school and all that. If you just wanna call round the garage after that, I'll check her over good and proper while you're workin' at the clinic today. I'll just get you to sign off the repairs now, so we don't have to worry about any more paperwork later. Does that work for you, lassie?"

"Um…but I didn't… I mean, I hadn't even…"

The old man's eyes crinkle at my lost expression and mindless ramblings. Moving closer, he hands over a clipboard with a pen attached. I look down at the paperwork, then back to him, my frown deepening. "I was going to call you this morning to get you to take a look at it and quote me on the repairs. Maybe see if you'd let me come to some sort of payment arrangement with you. But now, you're here, and I... " I'm lost for words, my heart thumping hard against my chest and my throat threatening to close shut, it's so tight. *How on earth am I going to afford this now?*

"No need. All taken care of. Now you're not caught without transport. It was no trouble."

"Well it *is*, Rob, because I don't even know how much this costs."

His brows bunch together. "Costin' you nothin', lassie. He took care of it." *He?* "Now just sign the invoice and I can leave you to your mornin'. Don't worry about the paperwork now, just bring it in with you when you call by the garage. See you then," he says, handing me the paper from the clipboard and my keys before stepping back and throwing me a wave over his shoulder as he moves back toward his truck and hops in.

Then I'm left staring at my truck in disbelief. Do I suddenly have a fairy godmother—well, *man*—or something? Because there's no way on this earth I'm *this* fortunate.

Curiosity has me glancing down at the invoice in my hand, my eyes skimming over the information before all the breath in my body rushes out of me and I stop breathing.

Because it seems I *do* have someone to thank for this, of the fairy god*father* variety, and his name is Beau Barnes.

Now it seems I have another stop to make on my way to work this morning because there's no way I'm letting that man pay for my repairs. I get that he's trying to be kind, but it goes against all that I am to accept a hand out of any kind—and Beau *knows* that. I'm not sure if I'm angry or embarrassed right now, but as I hop into the truck, my only hope is that I figure that out before I get there.

## 4

## BEAU

"Close the gate! Close the gate!" I yell at Sawyer, who's stopped to look over his shoulder at the sounds of an engine approaching in the distance. Gertie the goat makes a dive for the narrow opening, but thankfully my shouts snap Sawyer into action in time. If that goat got out of the pasture, I was likely to knock him in the side of his dumb blond head. Gertie is a hat and shoe-eating nightmare whenever she gets loose. If you ask our sister, Ellie-Mae, she'll rattle off a list of destroyed goods as long as her arm. If it wasn't for the fact that goats are natural weed clearers, she'd have been cooked up in a stew by now.

"Ha, ha! You're stuck, Gertie," Sawyer yells, but his laughter quickly stops when the goat lowers her head and looks ready to ram. That sends Sawyer hightailing it over the fence like a bat outta hell and me wishing I had my phone out to film it all.

"You look like you're practicin' to be a rodeo clown there, brother," I say as I follow him over the fence with a little more grace since he pretty much dove over it head first.

He scowls and dusts the dirt off his sleeve. "Never catch me bein' a clown. I last the full eight seconds every time," he spouts, mighty proud of his rodeo record and finding a chance to drop a mention of it whenever he can.

"Eight seconds, hey? The girls must love that," I tease with a chuckle, because while Sawyer loves to brag, we love to rib him every chance we get. It's just something brothers do.

"Shut the hell up. I'll have you know I'm virile as fu—"

"Molly's here," I say, taking my working gloves off and slapping them against his chest. "Finish up, will you?"

He mutters something about being treated like a clown on his own damn ranch. But I don't really listen because I'm jogging toward the ranch house where Molly is parking her truck. I can't believe it's up and running already. I only put a call into Rob this morning to ask him to take a look at it. Sure, I may have mentioned that she'd need it to get the kids to school, but I didn't expect him to be finished with it already. Then again, he's been maintaining all of our machines on the ranch for years now, even back when Dad was alive. He's never been one to muck around.

Molly cuts the engine just as I reach the car, but the smile I'm wearing to greet her quickly fades when I spot the steaming mad look on her face as she gets out and slams the door. I actually wince a little at the sound.

"Guessin' you're not out here to say thanks?" I say, placing my hands on my hips as she rounds the car like a tiny little tornado coming straight at me. She's adorable when she's mad, by the way.

"For embarrassin' me like that? When Rob came, I had no idea what was goin' on. And then it turns out this is all organized and paid for by one of the Barnes brothers. Do you have any idea how people are gonna be talkin' now? What do you think they're gonna say is goin' on between us after you did somethin' like that for me, Beau? One of the things I hold dear is my womanly pride, and *this* does not look particularly prideful."

"It was nothin'," I say straight away, trying not to smirk at the way she juts up her chin and her hands shoot up to rest on her slender hips. "No money exchanged hands at all. All I did was call in a favor. You're welcome, by the way."

Molly's sparking hazel eyes bug out, her mouth opening then slamming shut again as she splutters in disbelief. "A favor? What kind of favor gets you an early morning emergency repair *and* tow?"

"The kind where I gave that man's son a job last summer when no one else would have him."

She frowns slightly. "You talkin' about his older boy? The one who had some trouble with the law?"

"I am. He's joined the military now, but Rob credits his work on the ranch for straightening the kid out and givin' him direction. So he said he owed me a favor."

"OK. Then I guess I owe you a favor too."

I chuckle and fold my arms across my chest. "I don't need a favor from you, Molly. You've got enough on your plate as it is. Consider it being neighborly."

"I knew it!" She points her finger out in triumph. "You *did* do it 'cause you feel sorry for me."

"I did it because I wanted to help out a friend and it was in my power to do so. That's what you wanted, isn't it? To be *friends*?" My eyes travel down her figure, wishing we were anything but. Molly is beautiful and smart, and beyond all that, she makes me laugh and I genuinely enjoy spending time with her. If it wasn't for the fact she's overtaxed for time due to the care of her siblings and working so much, I'd have asked for far more than friendship months ago. But a man has to respect where a woman is coming from before he goes all caveman on her. So friends it is... for now, anyway.

Taking in a deep breath, she lets her shoulders drop. "Yeah," she says, her palm gently touching her forehead as she glances back to the truck and worries her lip between her teeth. "But friends or not, I can't accept this without doing something in return to pay you back. Don't get me wrong, I thank you from the bottom of my heart, Beau, and it was an amazing thing you did for me. But for me to feel right in acceptin' your kindness, I'm gonna need to either pay you back, or work it off. You choose."

Now it's my turn to look dumbfounded. "Can't ask you to do that, Molly. You work yourself into the ground as it is. When would you even find the time?"

"I'm free during the day most weekends. And when the kids aren't playin' sport, I can bring them too. Four sets of hands will work ]the debt off faster, right? And you never know, getting his hands dirty might give Colson some direction too."

As her eyes lift to mine, all I can see is tiredness and worry mixed with a determination to stand her ground, and even though I want to fight on her this and tell her that she will never, ever owe me a damn thing, I also can't turn her or her siblings away. Not when she's offering me something I actually want from her, something that she's short of and something that I'll treat as precious —time.

"OK," I say, holding out my hand to shake on our newly reached agreement. "Be here bright and early Saturday morning. I'll get y'all clearin' out the barn or somethin'."

"Thank you!" Beaming, she bypasses my outstretched hands and hugs me. It's so short and sweet that I don't even have time to react, but I feel it. There's no damn way I can't *not* feel it. The sensation of her all over, a spark of awareness that seems to run deep down into my soul, like it knows it's met its match. Possibly even its other half. *Thump. Thump. Thump.*

When she pulls away from me, my arms feel incredibly empty. "You won't regret this, Beau. We're gonna be the greatest ranch hands you've ever had." Molly backs away with a wide smile and gets in her truck, shooting me a wave before she backs out and turns her truck toward home. And as I watch her go I can't help but answer her even though she can't hear me.

"I could never regret anything with you, Molly Roberts."

"C'mon, guys. It's time to hit the road," I call out from the kitchen where I'm clearing away the last of the breakfast dishes.

In truth, I'm a whirlwind of nerves and excitement, and I'm channeling those feelings into my chores because today we're heading to Eagle Mountain Ranch to start working off my debt to Beau. And the nerves have absolutely nothing to do with the fact that I was still feeling tingles for hours after the impromptu hug I gave Beau yesterday. *Nothing at all...*

The added bonus is the fact I'm dragging the kids along with me and using this whole experience as a teaching exercise, showing them that although they didn't *mean* for the car to break down, they still took it without permission. So they need to learn that there are consequences to their actions—be it good or bad ones. In this case, we're all going to work on the ranch to repay Beau's kindness. Because I won't stand having it any other way. Stubborn pride or pig-headedness be damned. My kids, my car, my responsibility. We pay our way in this family.

I was so glad when Beau gave in to my demand that I pay him back for the repairs with farm labor. It's helped me accept what he did and become right with it. It was so incredibly kind and touching, but I'd much rather work myself into the ground than accept a handout, no matter who it's from. However, it's not exactly a hardship hanging out at the ranch with the Barnes family and my bestie, Kendra. Even Ellie-Mae, her husband Miller, and their cute little baby are fun to be around. And while I don't have time for dating or a relationship, ogling cowboys is probably my number one favorite thing to do. So really, I should owe them twice. But I think I'll keep that second part to myself—only so many hours in the day and all that.

"What do ya think?" Cody runs out, skidding to a stop in front of me and rendering me speechless, because he's dressed head to toe in cowboy *every-thing*—well everything he could lay his hands on by the looks of it. From jeans one size too small, to the big, bulky belt wrapped around his hips with a garish buckle that I recognize from Colson's Halloween costume a few years ago—including an oversized hat to boot, and then one of Dad's old flannel shirts he claimed when we sorted through the master bedroom. My eyes burn at this glimpse of the little kid part of Cody and my heart swells.

I cross my arms over my chest and look him up and down before nodding my approval. "I think you're ready for a day at the ranch working in the dirt with the cowboys."

"Good," he says as he turns his head and spots Sage and Colson coming toward us. "Last one to the car is a rotten egg! I call shotgun." Then he's off out the door, running to get the front seat like a loon.

Sage turns my way and quirks a brow, her lips twitching. "Does he *know* the doors are locked or should we just let him find out or himself?"

"He'll learn," Colson says, grabbing the pre-poured travel mug off the counter and giving me a chin lift before following after our youngest brother.

"You ready to work?" I ask Sage, quirking a brow at the trainers she's got on her feet.

"As I'll ever be," she says.

"You don't think you should have a pair of boots on for this?"

"Why? Won't we just be sweeping barns and shit?"

I hand Sage her own pink mug and grab mine before hooking my arm around her shoulder and leading her outside. "Oh girl, y'all have no idea. *So* much work goes into ranching. But that's what makes this all the more necessary. Hard work ain't ever hurt nobody, and maybe getting out in the fresh mountain air and sweatin' a little will be good for the soul. But you should really change your shoes."

The look she shoots me is full of disbelief. "Whatever, Molly," she mumbles against her coffee cup as she heads straight for the front door, ignoring me.

I smirk. "It's your funeral."

"Sooner we get this over and done with, the sooner I can get back here and relax," she calls over her shoulder.

I grab my keys and follow her out. "Oh, did I not mention there are still chores to be done around home too."

She drops her head back with a groan. "Ugh. Never gonna eat ice cream again."

It's *then* that I giggle and shake my head as I lock up the house and slip behind the steering wheel. Destination, Eagle Mountain Ranch...and Beau...

I PULL the truck to a stop in the big dirt parking area outside the ranch house just as Kendra, Jesse, and Ellie-Mae are walking out the front door, Ellie's wriggling toddler, Whitney, in her arms.

"Hey, y'all," Ellie-Mae says with a welcoming smile as Kendra makes her way over and gives me a big hug before doing the same to the kids, who are all surprisingly quiet beside me. "Beau said you were coming by today, I didn't expect the kids to come along too." Her brown eyes assess me, but there's no missing her unspoken question.

"Yeah. Well, I figure they can't get into any trouble out here on the ranch. And many hands make short work, right? Isn't that what they say, Jesse?"

He grins as he rakes his fingers through his dark beard. "Oh yeah. You can never have enough helpers on a ranch, especially when the work never ends and the animals are never *not* hungry."

"Whoa. We can *feed* them? Like, by hand?" Cody asks, his voice full of wonder.

"Sure can, cowboy." Jesse moves to Cody's side and shucks the lip of his hat with his thumb. "And since you're already dressed the part, you're all set to be my helper today if ya want."

Cody's head snaps my way, his eyes pleading for me to say yes. I shrug. "Sounds good to me. You just listen to what Jesse says and do exactly what he tells you to do, yeah?"

He rushes my way and gives me a quick hug. "You're the best, Molly."

"I know." I shrug and grin down at him. "Means I can keep an eye on your brother and sister here. Can't have them shirking off on the job now, can we?"

Cody pokes his tongue out at our siblings before slowing his gait as he moves back to Jesse's side, the man meeting my gaze. "Beau's expectin' you. He just went to clean up in the bunkhouse. You're welcome to go see him or—"

"No. No. It's OK. I mean..." I swallow down my *slight* panic and take a deep, calming breath. "We can just wait here for him. Wouldn't want to interrupt anything or—"

Jesse chuckles, his eyes dancing with amusement as he wraps an arm around Kendra's shoulders and pulls her in close to his side. She tips her head and smiles up at him just as he touches his lips to hers and I have to bite back a hopeless sigh, so glad that my best friend has found her one and only. I've told her many a time that theirs is the exact type of love story I love to read—like the ones my favorite author, Aster Hollingsworth, writes about.

"See you later, doc?" Jesse drawls.

"You know you will, cowboy," she hums before they kiss goodbye one last time and Jesse jerks his chin Cody's way.

"You like horses, bud?"

"Sure!"

"Then let me introduce you to my pal, Buster. He just loves people. Especially kids with cool belt buckles."

"For real?"

"Yep."

"Whoa. I'm glad I put this on then. Do you reckon I can pet him?"

"I have a feelin' you'll be doin' more than that. How are you are sittin' on saddles?" Cody squeals and starts jumping instead of walking as they move toward the barn and out of sight.

Kendra moves to stand by my side while Colson laughs at how much Sage is cooing over Whitney.

"You sure about this whole working here to pay back the repair bill?" Kendra asks under her breath. "I worry about how much you're working, Molls."

"I'm positive. I can't have Beau callin' in favors for me. We're not kin." She opens her mouth to argue, and I know she's going to make a speech about him being her family and therefore mine because we're best friends, but I beat her to it. "*Still*, I appreciate what he did—I'm not so proud that I can't see his intentions were good—but I live and breathe knowing that I'm raising those kids right. You don't take handouts unless you're gonna pay it forward and working here, helping out, that's us all doing that."

"Molly, you know you're family to us too. We see you working yourself into the ground and just want to make things easier for you in any way we can."

"And I appreciate that more than you know, Kendie. This is just something I want to do. Beau gets that, that's why he agreed to let me work off the bill."

"Yeah, *sure* that's the only reason," she murmurs under her breath. "Nothing to do with the fact you get to spend time with your favorite cowboy or anything."

I pretend I didn't hear her, let alone acknowledge the truth in her statement. *A girl's allowed to look and not touch, right? Even if touching is definitely something I wish I could do...*

"What was that?" I ask, my lips curving up.

Kendra shakes her head. "Nuthin," she says before her eyes lift up and crinkle at the sides. "Speak of the devil." Her tone is weird, almost wistful, with a tinge of excitement.

"Beau's no dev-" I stop mid-sentence as I look over in the direction of the bunkhouse and suddenly become thankful I'm leaning up against the truck because lord, almighty, I'm not sure I can put into words just how yummy Beau Barnes is looking today.

He's wearing a wife-beater tank with an open red flannel shirt over top, and blue denim jeans that are so tight on his thighs I'm hoping and praying that the material might be faulty because the image of the material bursting open and giving me a glimpse of what's underneath is suddenly high on the list of sights I'd like to see.

Beau's mouth tugs up on one side as he spots us, his long strides swallowing up the space as the swirling lust in my stomach swallows my ability to talk, think, maybe even breath.

A nudge against my arm knocks me out of my Beau-induced trance. When I turn my head, I'm met by a smirking Colson, gesturing to the corner of his mouth.

Frowning at him, his smirk widens. "Hey, Molls. You're drooling," he whispers, making me gasp.

"What? No. What?" I splutter, but instinctively rub my mouth, earning me a manly chuckle from my far-too-observant brother.

"Yeah. That's what I thought. It's all good, Molls. Your secret is safe with me," he says, leaning in and kissing my temple before straightening and grinning at Beau as he comes to a stop next to El-lie, Sage, and baby Whitney.

Then I have to lock my knees and think about anything that's *not* hot because Beau leans down and nuzzles his mouth against Whitney's chubby baby cheek, and I swear even Sage blushes at the show of ovary-obliterating cuteness.

And when Beau turns that smile my way, his warm brown eyes meeting mine before he makes a more than obvious, heat-inducing scan down my body and back up again.

Damn, has the weather changed or something? Cause all of a sudden it's hot as Hades.

"Ready to get to work?" he asks, clapping his hands together as he looks over the three of us, his eyes dropping to Sage's trainers. "Got some-thin' different to put on your feet, darlin'?"

"She's insisting they'll be fine since she's just 'sweeping barns and stuff'," I relay, using air quotes and enjoying the way Beau's eyes sparkle and his mouth twitches as he nods.

"Well then, I guess the young ones always know best. Come on then, Roberts family. Let's get on with this," Beau says, putting us straight to work without a fuss reminds me of the reason we're here. To work... just work. We're not here to perve on the ranchers—even if they do look like they've walked off the pages of the Cowboys of America calendar...

"Yep. Ready and willing here, Beau," I blurt, causing Beau to pause and look straight into my eyes. "Whatever you need, wherever you need it, we're here to do it." His brow goes up, and I falter. "Well, me and the kids are ready to...you know...do ranch stuff."

His lips twitch as he continues to stare straight into my eyes for so long that I start to squirm in my boots. Then, with a sharp jerk of his chin, he gets straight down to business.

"Right then. Follow me. Time to teach y'all the inner workings of Eagle Mountain Ranch. You know...ranch stuff," he adds with a wink.

## 6

## BEAU

"What the actual hell?" Sage cries, her entire foot getting caught in a fresh cow pat as we travel around the ranch, topping up water troughs.

"I did *tell* you to wear boots," Molly says, trying to keep a straight face. Colson doesn't even try to hide his laughter, especially when Sage dislodges her foot, but her trainer doesn't come with it.

"Oh god no!" she wails, dropping to her knees next to the animal dung and clutching the sides of her head. "What do I do?"

"You fish it out," I state, plain as day.

Her eyes go wide in horror. "With what?"

I hold my hand up and wiggle my fingers, to which she shakes her blonde head in resolute denial. "You can't expect me to touch that stuff!"

"Then I guess you're down a shoe." I shrug.

"It's OK, sis," Colson adds. "They were shit shoes, anyway." I try to hide my smirk, but that comment sets Molly off.

She tips her head back and howls with laughter, almost dropping to her knees as she clutches her belly and keeps repeating, 'Shit shoes!' before starting to laugh all over again. At first, Sage doesn't find it funny at all, but Molly goes on for so long that the rest of us end up laughing with her. And when I calm down, I realize that I've never seen her laugh that much. Ever. *But damn, what I wouldn't give to see her like this more often.*

"This is so gross," Sage claims after using the laces to fish her trainer out of the dung. It spins slowly on the end of the muddy-colored string. "You know, Cols. They're not just shit. They're totally fucked." Colson and Sage laugh together until Molly cuts in.

"Hey! Enough with the language."

"Sorry, but I can't put this back on my foot."

"You're right," I say, turning to Colson. "Why don't you take the Gator and your sister back to the ranch house? Ask Ellie-Mae if she can spare a set of boots then make your way back over here when you're done."

Colson's eyes light up. "You're trustin' me with the Gator?"

"You know how to drive, don't ya?"

"Well, yeah."

"Then off you go. Should only take about thirty minutes, round trip. No joy ridin'. Deal?"

"Yes, sir." Colson salutes, then heads to the Gator with his sister hopping along behind him.

"That's a lot of trust you're puttin' in a couple of kids there," Molly says when Colson lets out a 'yahoo' as they drive off.

"Not much trouble they can get into between here and the ranch house," I say, continuing along. "Randy and I used to have a riot in our first one of those. Feels like freedom. And I figure it's a lot better hoonin' around the ranch than on public roads."

"You think that's what they're missing?" she asks, quickening her pace a little to catch up to me. "Freedom?"

I turn and look at her for a long moment. "Aren't you?"

A soft gasp escapes her, and she stops walking for a second. But I continue along because I'm leading a herd of cattle right now who love to follow, since to them seeing a human means sustenance is coming. And they don't want to stop, because who doesn't like a nice cool drink on a warm day? I also don't feel like being crowded and knocked about by a group of large animals.

"Oh goodness," Molly yelps as she picks up the pace and runs to catch up to me. "Do they always do that?"

"Sure do."

She glances over her shoulder and smiles. "It's kinda cute. Like we're the pied piper of cattle."

"Fuckin' adorable," I say, not just talking about the cows.

We reach the little undercover area where the troughs are kept, and I get to work. This enclosed space is both to keep the water cool and drinkable in summer and to stop it from freezing over in the winter.

"Lucky the kids aren't around right now or I'd have to scold you for cussing too," she teases as I flip the faucet on and watch the water pour in. The cows moo and jostle to position themselves around it, stretching their necks to get the freshest water first.

"You can scold me whenever you like, angel. Can't say I'm gonna listen though. I'm a little too old to rein anythin' in anymore. And believe me, Ellie-Mae has tried many a time over the years."

"You are so not old, Beau Barnes," she retorts before a cow nuzzles her in the cheek then licks her under her chin. She giggles and I can't help but laugh at such a pure, joyous moment. "Gosh. They're so friendly and sweet."

"They live a good life here. Most animals are friendly when you treat 'em right."

"Even cowboys?"

I shut off the water as I smirk. "You callin' me an animal, Molly Roberts?"

She flicks some of the water from the trough at me. "You smell like one right now,"

"I'll bet you do too," I say, splashing some back. "Maybe I should disconnect this hose and wash you down right now?"

"Don't you dare, Beau Barnes!" she yelps, holding out her hands as she backs away while I make a show of pulling the hose from the connector. "I do *not* need to walk around in the heat with sopping wet jeans and boots." My dick suddenly likes the image of Molly Robert's soaked from head to toe, her clothes clinging to her curves.

"Well, if you run, my old man legs might not be fast enough to catch you." I lift the hose and flick some water at her. She shrieks and jumps out of the way.

"Oh my god, you're not old!" She's laughing now and fuck does it feel good to be the one making her smile.

"Next to you and your siblings, I'm fuckin' ancient."

"Well, you've got a mouth on you like an old sailor."

"Fuckin' oath, I do." I flick the water again and she jumps to the side again, laughing until she collides with the flank of a particularly thirsty cow and bounces right off, losing her footing and falling flat on her back.

My eyes go wide and I throw the hose to the side, rushing to help her up before she gets inadvertently stomped on.

"Holy shit, angel. I'm so fucking sorry," I say, grabbing her arms and hauling her to her feet. "You OK?" I place my hands on either side of her head and look deep into her eyes, making sure her pupils are the same size, and that she didn't hit her head and get a concussion or something. "Molly?"

"Beau." Her whisper catches me off guard as her eyes lift to mine. It's then that I realize she was just staring at my mouth. A frown creases my brow as I caress her cheek lightly with my thumb, loving the feel of her silky smooth skin under mine. She leans into me. *Well, fuck.*

She either hit her head real hard, or she actually wants to kiss me. I lick my lips, so badly hoping it's the latter because there's nothing I want more than to press my mouth to hers, to taste her sinful pink lips and remember what it's like to have someone as young and vibrant as Molly in my arms. But then reality kicks in and I remember back to our night at the Lair months ago and her insistence that she wasn't looking for any kind of relationship. And since I'm not the kind of guy who takes advantage of a woman in any state—exhausted or otherwise—I swallow down my own desires and slowly let her go, putting a couple of feet's worth of distance between us.

"I'm sorry you fell," I say, my voice thick and rough as I pick the hose up and take the time to reattach it again, using the break to get my head screwed on straight. "I shoulda known better than to fuck around near a bunch of thirsty cows. You coulda been hurt and that's on me. You're bringin' your siblings around here to teach them about the world, and well, I'm old enough to know better."

"You seem really hung up on how old you are, Beau. I'm fine. All my fingers and toes are intact and we were havin' fun. You forget that *I'm* old enough to know better too. But if I've learned anything over the past few years, it's that some-times it's good to forget how grown up you really are and just let loose once in a while, don't you think? At the end of the day, we're all just a bunch of kids at heart. Life is too short to be quiet and serious all the time."

"You can't work all the time, either," I point out, feeling eternally worried about her, constantly fighting against a desperate longing to scoop her up and carry her load for a spell, even though I know she won't let me. She won't let anyone. She's so strong and stubborn, and I both admire and feel frustrated by it. Because at the end of the day, while she's watching over everyone, who's looking after her?

Molly gives me a half-hearted smile. "I don't re-ally have a choice in that at the moment. But that's why I do all my socializing and fun-having on the job. Up there for thinkin', Beau." She taps her head as a dry laugh passes her lips. "And speaking of work, I think I can hear that Gator in the distance. Maybe we should get back to it be-fore the kids get back here and catch us slackin' off."

"Yeah. But it's good to see you relax a little, Molls. You should laugh more often."

She looks up at me and smiles. "Yeah? Maybe I should get a job at a day spa or somethin'?"

"That's not quite what I meant," I say with a roll of my eyes.

"I know. But it's the only way it's gonna happen," she says, bouncing her shoulders before she turns and walks back into the paddock to greet her siblings returning in the Gator with clean boots, some food, and smiles on their faces. In some ways, I feel kind of proud of those smiles because it was my actions that brought them all here so they could experience something greater than the daily grind. And now, more than ever, I'm starting to think that maybe I *am* the man Molly needs, it's just up to me to prove that to her. The only way I'm going to do that is through my actions. She doesn't need a hero, she needs a partner, someone to stand beside her and support her, someone she knows will never let her fall. And right now, every bone in my body is telling me that I'm the only man put on this earth to be that for her. So that's exactly what I'm doing to do, whatever it takes, however long it takes me.

## 7

## MOLLY

I t's been hours since we got home from the ranch, yet my entire body, every inch of my skin, has been buzzing where Beau's big strong hands touched me. I don't know what he saw in my expression, but I felt the loss of him the second he stepped back. Just that one moment had me so mesmerized I was barely able to stay upright. And when his skin touched mine, the jolt of awareness that catapulted through me was almost overwhelming.

Actually, there was no *almost* about it. It's like his touch was akin to me poking my finger into a power outlet and holding on for the ride—it was crazy, inexplicable, and it well and truly succeeded in throwing all of my reasons why I shouldn't get close to Beau out the window.

Even now, as I run the events of the day over and over in my head while getting ready for my shift at the Lair, I can't seem to pinpoint what the hell happened. I lost my footing. I fell over. I *may* have lost focus for a spell because I was watching Beau a little too closely, one of many looks I'd been sneaking at the man while in his presence.

My heart feels like I've run a marathon too, and even though we did work hard today, this is a different kind of exhaustion. Not from overdoing things, more like from my pulse racing every single time Beau would just *look* at me. Or get close. And when he touched me, lord... I swear I almost fainted because my blood ran so hot I thought I was at risk of self-combusting. Then it was like a switch was flicked off and he went back to being the concerned *friend* worried that I was working myself too hard. *Sigh*. And I thought *I* was hot and cold!

I shake my head as I lean in close to the mirror to swipe some mascara on. I must have a screw loose and be imagining things. Maybe knowing I want him but not allowing myself to even *consider* having him is muddling my mind.

Having applied one layer, I straighten and assess my reflection. I have my mousey blonde hair tied up in a high pony today and I've curled it so there are cute little flicks at the ends. And I'm wearing my Lion's Lair tee paired with black jeans and my black sneakers that are so well worn, they're the only shoes I have that don't have my feet hurting by the end of a long shift.

For a moment, I look myself over head to toe and wonder what Beau thinks when he sees me. I *know* he's interested in me, and whenever we're close he makes it clear that I have his whole attention in that moment. It's thrilling, and it's definitely more than a little flattering, but it's also damn scary... in a good way. Because I could so easily fall for him, and it's not the first time I've become worried that I'm denying myself something good... something *life-changing,* by locking Beau Barnes firmly in the friend zone.

I spritz myself with my favorite vanilla and jasmine-scented perfume, letting the fragrance fill my senses. I don't usually go all out for my bar shifts, but something has me wanting to put a little effort in tonight. Not only does it pick me up and give me an extra pep in my step, but I'd be lying if I said I wasn't thinking about the chance of seeing Beau again tonight. He and his brothers are Lair regulars, so the likelihood is quite high. I gasp as butterflies flutter in my tummy and my heart does a happy flip at the thought.

"What're you grinning about, Molls?" Colson says, leaning a shoulder into the bathroom doorway.

I jump at his voice and press my hand to my chest as a shriek of surprise escapes me. "Dude, don't sneak up on me like that."

My brother snorts and shakes his head. "Yeah right. I could tell you were away with the fairies. What are you thinking about? Or is it more of a case of *who*?" There's no missing his singsong teasing tone.

I poke my tongue out at him. "Stop it. There's nothin' going on."

"I know. Doesn't mean you don't want there to be, 'cause there's no missin' the way Beau Barnes was lookin' at ya today."

"Eww, Cols. No. I'm so not talkin' to you about dating."

"Ah. So you're *datin'* now? Here was I thinking you two just had the hots for one another"

"What? No. I mean..." I clamp my mouth shut and shake my head.

"*Now* I get it. You *want* to..."

"N—shit." I turn toward him and press a hip to the vanity. "My focus is on you kids and providing for and supporting you all. That's it. I'll have plenty of time to have a love life with dates and all of that once you're all grown up and not needing me anymore."

"That's where you're wrong, Molls."

My brows bunch together. "What do you mean?"

"I mean I don't see the sense in waitin' 'cause there ain't ever gonna be a time when we don't need you. It'll just be in a different way. Just like I hope the same goes for you needing the three of us. We're family, and family is *always* there for one another, right?"

"You've got a good head on your shoulders, you know that?"

"Oh yeah. Learned from the best. But I did wanna talk to you about somethin'."

"You've got my attention. What's up?"

"I truly am sorry about the car, and I would've walked a hundred dogs if it meant you don't have to work yourself into the ground to pay for the repairs."

"Cols, it's OK. I'm well and truly over that now. The cars fixed and we're paying for it by working as a team."

"Yeah, but that's the thing. As much as I regret it, I also don't, 'cause workin' at the ranch isn't a punishment to me. I actually really like it."

My head jerks back. "Really?"

He shrugs, like his admission isn't a big deal, but to me, it's *huge*. "Yeah. It was interestin'. And Beau and his brothers are cool. Sawyer was telling us all about the rodeo and the places he's been, then Randy and Miller talked about this big homestead on Bear mountain where they're all about protectin' the environment and living off the land but givin' back to it too." There's no mistaking the interest in Colson's words. He's not just telling me this because he thinks I want to hear it, he's being completely genuine, like he's finally gotten a glimpse of the path he wants to walk in life.

"Yeah. Kendra has told me about it before. She's even been up there once. Miller came from there, and he and Ellie-Mae visit whenever they can."

"It's not just all of that, though. I liked working with my hands and getting involved. Maybe I could, you know..."

"Learn more about ranching?"

His eyes perk up and oh yes, there's interest there. My brother might've just found his passion and maybe a future career he hadn't yet considered.

"Maybe then, instead of serving your time at the ranch working as punishment, you can use it as a chance to soak up all the knowledge from Beau, Jesse, and the other brothers. See what you need to learn at school, or what you can do at college to help you toward becoming a rancher."

"There's my sister, grabbing on to a morsel and making it into a meal," he says with a soft smirk, but I don't miss the gratitude in his gaze.

"Hey, when it comes to you, little brother, I'll take what I can get. I better finish getting ready otherwise I'll be late and then I'll miss out on tips that'll help buy you new cleats since football season is just around the corner."

"Love ya, Molls."

"Love you too, ya lug. Now, off with you. It's movie night, right? Popcorn, candy, and Cody's choice of Star Wars movie, no doubt."

"Marvel! We're doing a *Marvel* marathon, Molly. Jeez, don't you remember *anything*," Cody yells from down the hall.

I roll my eyes and Colson just grins, giving me a chin lift before disappearing toward the kitchen.

Then I finish my makeup, giving a little internal fist pump because one of my biggest worries about being the responsible adult and guardian for my siblings has been whether I was doing a good enough job at guiding them and preparing them for wherever their lives may take them.

And with Colson leaning towards ranching, my job now is to nurture that and keep encouraging him to pursue it.

I'm still running through all the different things I could do to help Colson learning about animal husbandry, working the land, ranch operations, and even just simple logistics involved in running a farming operation the likes of Eagle Mountain Ranch when I pull into the parking lot of the tavern, wondering why my skin has suddenly started tingling again.

Parking my truck in one of the delegated staff spots, I turn my head to see that the bar is already pumping, which means it'll be a busy night from now right through till closing time. It also means being too busy to clock watch, so it won't even feel like I'm working into the early hours after putting in a good amount of time and effort at the ranch today.

I grab my purse and lock up, then make my way to the front door, every step closer making me feel funny. It's not just tingles now either, my arms are covered in goosebumps, and all of my senses are suddenly super acute.

When my gaze lands on a very familiar-looking truck parked near the front porch, my heart joins the party and starts thumping along to its own excited beat, speeding up the closer I get to the door.

Any tiredness I *was* feeling vanishes into thin air because that truck means Beau is inside, and there's no way I can deny the butterflies in my tummy or the smile tugging at my lips.

Maybe it's time to stop lying to myself. So Colson was right, I have a crush on that man... but I'm a grown woman. I can have a crush and not act on it, not when I've vowed to myself to focus on the kids and *then* think about dating... way, way, *way* down the line.

Still, there's nothing wrong with a little harmless flirting, right?

And that's what I keep telling myself as I step inside the Lair and prepare myself to see, drool, and maybe even swoon, over Beau Barnes for the second time in a day.

## 8

## BEAU

"Here's to the end of another long week," Randy says, setting a tray of beer, wings, and curly fries down on the table between us all. Coming to the Lair is a bit of a tradition for us Barnes men. It's pretty much a tradition for most of Kinleyville since it's the only decent place near town to wet your whistle and kick your boots up—at the end of the working day. We're missing Jesse and our honorary brother, Miller, but since they're all coupled up, it's understandable they'd rather spend a night in with their Ones instead of coming to a noisy bar with the rest of us. And while the work week never really ends for us ranchers, the weekend still gets celebrated because we tend to keep to a light load on Sundays as best we can. That's as much of a day off as we get.

"And here's to long-legged women with tight jeans and loose belt buckles," Sawyer adds, lifting his glass as Randy slides into the booth next to him.

"You're gonna end up catchin' something if you keep goin' the way you are," Randy says with a shake of his head. "You're givin' the rest of us a bad name."

"Ah, I doubt that. The women 'round here already have their bouquets picked out in the hopes of landing one of you two."

"You don't think they'd do the same for you?" I ask, lifting my brow as I lift my beer to my lips.

Sawyer shakes his head and looks over to the dancefloor where a group of women are starting to line up. "I'm not the marryin' kind."

Randy and I exchange amused looks. "Might wanna tell the mountain that," Randy says with a smirk. "From what Jesse and Miller say, when your Call comes, there ain't nothin' you can do to stop it." *The Call...*

My brow knits as I set my beer on the table, then chew on some curly fries thoughtfully. "This Call," I start, once I've swallowed my food. "Exactly how do you know it's arrived?"

Randy's head pulls back slightly and Sawyer's ears perk up, his attention swinging back to me. "You're fuckin' hearin' it, ain't cha?"

Placing my fingers on the top of my glass, I turn it slightly and shake my head. "Never said that. Just wanna know how to tell when it's here. Ain't nothing wrong with bein' inquisitive last I checked."

Sawyer laughs like he doesn't believe a word I'm saying and goes back to scanning the crowd, looking for his bed partner for the night. But Randy at least takes my inquiry seriously.

"I don't know exactly what it's like since I haven't felt it. But from what I hear, it's like you get real hot, like electricity is buzzin' beneath your skin. And your heart beats real hard, like your body is tellin' ya that your soulmate is comin' near. Then as you get closer, that bond grows stronger and you're like, connected or somethin' and can't be away from each other. Miller and Jesse can both tell you more about *that* particular part of it if you ask 'em. But I reckon it has to be true just by watchin' the way they are with their Ones. And don't forget that Kendra is our mountain's seer. If the Call is comin' your way, she can guide you and let you know if what you're experiencin' 'round young Molly is the real deal or not."

"I never said I was experincin' anythin'," I retort, lifting my beer and drinking almost half of it down. "Molly's made it crystal clear that friend-ship is all she has time for right now, and I'm in-clined to respect that."

Randy smirks behind his glass. "Call don't give a shit about timin', brother. It pushes you together when the Mountain Spirit feels there's a reason for the Call to be sounded."

"Well, sometimes the Mountain Spirit might have to wait, because there's no way I'm puttin' any extra pressure on that girl when she's already—"

"So, you *are* hearin' the Call," Sawyer interjects with a big shit-eating grin on his face.

I roll my eyes and shake my head. "I fuckin' never said that. And even if I did, she isn't interested. She said as much herself the one and only time we went on a date."

"Thought that night was just friends hangin' out," Sawyer teases.

"That's all it ended up bein'," I say, picking up a wing so I can eat and stop this interrogation. "So, that's what it—" I stop talking mid-sentence as my skin heats suddenly, and as if drawn like a beacon, my eyes lift to the entry doors of the Lair. I don't even need to be told who it is because I already know who's about to walk through. *Molly*.

Thump. Thump. Thump.

Lowering my gaze, I try to go back to what I was saying so my brothers don't realize what's caught my attention, but it's already too late. Sawyer has turned back to me with laughter in his eyes. "Just ask the girl out," he says, tearing up a wing with his fingers as he shakes his head. "You obviously want her."

"What I want and what she needs are two very different things," I say, going back to my food. "I ain't gonna force it. I'm not that guy."

It's then that Molly spots us at our table and gives me a shy little finger wave.

*Thump. Thump. Thump.*

"All I'm seein' is a sweet little thing who both needs *and* wants you, brother," Sawyer says as he licks ranch off his fingers. "And if you're not gonna do somethin' about it. Then I will."

"Stay the hell out of it," Randy barks, giving Sawyer an elbow to the side. "The Spirit knows what She's doin' and we've gotta trust that. She hasn't steered anyone wrong so far, so I don't expect Her to start now. Just let nature run its course, like in all things we do. You feel me, brother?" He gives Sawyer a long look of warning before Sawyer scowls and nods, grumbling under his breath.

"Fine. But if you let that girl slip through your fingers, it'll be on you."

"Well, if she slips through my fingers it won't have been the Call now, will it?" I retort before I sit back and frown. "Unless the Call can be one-sided?"

Randy frowns. "I don't think so. But maybe run that one by Kendra. She'll know for sure."

I lift my beer and look over to where Molly is tying her apron around her waist at the start of her shift. "Maybe I will talk to Kendra," I say, taking a sip before realizing my drink is empty.

Randy laughs. "Bit distracted there, brother? Must be time for another?"

"I'll get them," I say, ignoring the look my brothers exchange before I make my way across the crowded room to Molly.

*Thump. Thump. Thump.*

"Howdy, partner," she says with a smile when it's my turn at the bar. "What can I get you?"

I scrub a hand across the stubble on my face to hide the grin that takes over the moment I lock eyes with hers. Maybe this *is* the Call—it wouldn't be the first time I've wondered. But maybe it's something else instead. Whatever it is, there's just something about this girl that makes me happy just being near her.

"Another round for me and my brothers, thanks." I reach into my back pocket to pull my wallet out as she collects the glasses. "Gotta admit, I kinda hoped I wouldn't see you here tonight, angel." I hand over the twenty as her eyebrows shoot up, but I keep going before she can protest. "Only 'cause you've been on your feet all day and I worry 'bout you drivin' home exhausted on those dark roads."

Her expression softens immediately. "You don't have to worry about me, Beau Barnes."

"Of course I do," I say, clearing my throat as she picks up a glass and lifts it to the tap, flipping the lever so the foamy beer comes out and clears. She keeps her eyes on me, though. *Why am I feeling so hot all of a sudden?* "We're friends, right? Friends worry."

She sets the first drink in front of me with a resigned sigh. "Yeah. Friends worry. And I appreciate you carin'. I also appreciate how much patience you showed with me and the kids today. Colson really enjoyed the experience. Cody too. But you have Colson *really* excited. I don't think I've seen him so interested in something since before Dad died. So, I must thank you for that. I think being at the ranch was the highlight of everyone's day." The second beer lands in front of me and she moves to the last one.

"I'm happy to hear that. There's always plenty of work to do on the ranch, so any time they want the experience, we're more than happy to oblige."

"For real?" Her brows shoot up for the second time in the conversation, but this time the accompanying expression is a lot more favorable.

I lift my beer and take a sip as I chuckle. "For real," I repeat, realizing that this right here—giving the kids a place to go so she's not always worrying about them—could be the thing I can do to ease her burden. "How about this? If you can get Colson up early, I can swing by and take him out to the ranch for the day. Get him doing some real work. Maybe start showing him what we have to do day-to-day to keep the ranch running like a well-oiled machine."

"You sayin' that wasn't real work we did today?" She places the final beer in front of me, then moves to process the sale. "I hope you weren't goin' easy on me, Beau."

"Never, angel," I say with a wink as she tries to hand me my change. I collect the beers and wave her off and thankfully she doesn't argue. *For once.* "Just tell him I'll come collect him bright and early."

"OK." She smiles. "I'll give him a call and tell him on my break. Thanks so much, Beau. He's gonna be so excited."

"My pleasure, Molly," I say, nodding in place of tipping my hat as all manner of more *pleasurable* things I could do with his girl bounce around inside my head. "I'll see you tomorrow."

"Look forward to it," she says as I turn away and head back to my brothers, struggling to keep the grin off my face because this just means I'll be seeing Molly more and more. And finally, I'm doing something to help her too.

What she doesn't yet know is that I'm gonna keep doing it. That's what *friends* do after all.

## 9

# MOLLY

"**M**ollllyyyyy! You've got a *visitorrrrrr...*" Sage calls out, disturbing me from my solitude as I snuggle under my comforter and steal a few moments of peace, rereading one of my favorite Aster Hollingsworth books. I figure, since I won't let myself live out my own cowboy fantasies, I might as well lose myself in a fictional one instead.

"Take care of it, Sage!" I call back without thinking.

"It's *Beaaaaauuuuu!*" This time my entire body goes still before I jump into action, my mind going from lazy and relaxed to freaking out and panicked in the blink of an eye. I don't think I've ever moved as fast as I am jumping out of bed and whirling around like a human tornado, trying to find something...*anything*, to wear that's even remotely good enough to be seen in at short notice by *Beau*.

"I'll be out in a jiffy!" *Who the hell says jiffy? I must've been hanging out with the old folks too much?*

"You're *such* a doofus, Molly. How on earth did you *forget*," I scold myself, jumping on one leg and hopping to and fro, struggling to pull up a pair of black leggings with one hand and raking my fingers through my bed hair with the other.

I swear this entire situation would almost be funny if it was anyone else waiting for me, not the man who seems to be consuming my thoughts of late.

Once I've quickly put on a bra and pulled my favorite 'Mountain Men Do it Better' hoodie I bought from an online book merch store as a treat, I take one last glance in the mirror, then paint a cool, calm, pretending-to-be-relaxed smile on my face and move down the hall.

When I reach the living area, I find Sage giggling and grinning at Beau, Cody sitting beside him looking at the man like he hung the moon for him, and Colson cradling a coffee mug in his hand as he leans back against the kitchen counter, looking *far* older than I'm ready to admit he is.

"Hey," I say, making my presence known as all eyes swing to me. Beau's are soft and warm, like melted chocolate you just wanna bathe in as they look me over. "Sorry I wasn't up. I forgot you were coming so early."

His lips curve up as he shoots me a wink. "No rest for the wicked, angel."

*Damn, is it hot in here?* Maybe I'm coming down with something, because I swear Beau is *flirting* with me and I'm *totally* not equipped or caffeinated enough to deal with an even hotter, cuter, more irresistible Beau Barnes so soon after waking.

"Glad you remembered, Cols. Got everything you need?"

"Yeah. I was up with the sun," he says, sipping his coffee and earning a nod of approval from Beau. My heart swells a little at the interaction.

Cody bounces on the couch excitedly. "Beau was telling us how Gertie the goat ran away with one of Randy's boots, and Randy and Sawyer were chasing her around the paddock for *half an hour* while the goat was gnawing on the leather like a tasty snack!" he practically yells.

Colson shakes his head with a smirk. "I'm surprised he doesn't end up as goat stew."

"Eww. Gross, Cols." Sage twists up her face in disgust before turning to Beau. "You wouldn't do that, right?" Sage asks "You wouldn't eat him... would you?"

Cody jumps right in with an answer. "Don't you know, Sage? Everything on a ranch gets used and reused, including animals."

Beau glances down at Cody and ruffles his hair. "You seem to know a bit about ranchin', little man. You been learning a few things at school?"

"Nope. Been readin' up about how to become a cowboy!"

Beau chuckles. "That's the spirit. And when Colson gets back from the ranch today, he can tell you all about it. Expand your knowledge and all."

"Oooh, can I come too? I promise to be good and listen to everything you tell me to. Will Jesse be there as well? And Sawyer? And that tall dude who keeps losing his hat in the wind?" Cody word vomits, his excitement a lot more obvious than his brother's, who's obviously trying to play it cool in front of his new hero.

Beau rests his hand on Cody's shoulder and squeezes it. "Sure thing." Beau's gaze shifts to meet mine. "If it's OK with your sister, of course."

Cody jumps off the couch and runs straight for me, scooping my hands in his and sending me his best puppy dog eyes. "Pleeeaaassseee, Molly. I promise to be good and do *all* my chores and be on my *best* behavior…"

I hem and haw, making a show of it and drawing it out until Cody is near on vibrating with desperation for my answer. I turn him around and wrap my arms around his chest, dipping my head to rest on his shoulder as I look over to an amused-looking Colson and Beau. "What do you think, guys? Is Cody big enough to work the ranch with y'all?"

I bite back a laugh as Cody's head nods up and down against mine.

Proving he's a good sport and *not* an old fart like he seems to think he is, Beau lifts his hand and rubs his chin.

"You got a hat?" he continues.

"Yes, sir."

Beau arches a brow. "A *real* cowboy hat this time? If you're gonna be a legit rancher, you need a real hat on your head."

Cody's breath catches and he goes to shake his head before he stills and nods even *more* excitedly than before. "Yes, sir. I have my daddy's hat in the garage."

My chest seizes with pride, my throat growing tight with emotion as I look over to find Sage smiling, her eyes glassy as she bites her lip, trying to keep a hold on her feelings.

"Well then, as long as you're willin' to work hard like I expect all the men on our ranch to do, then I'd love to have another set of hands to help us today."

"Yes!" Cody says, wriggling free and pumping his fist in the air. "I better get ready." Then he's gone, leaving us all in his dust.

"That OK with you?" Beau asks, taking a sip of his coffee in front of him.

"Me? Fine by me. You sure you wanna take on not one but *two* Roberts boys today?"

"I think they'll do fine."

"Um... Are Roberts's *girls* welcome? Because I'd love to help Ellie-Mae with the bakin' Whitney again. That was fun," Sage says, sounding almost meek and shy, totally not like my sister.

"Sure thing, Sage. Might be good to give your sister a day to herself, yeah?"

I splutter, the thought of having an entire day to myself not even registering until now. "What?" I whisper. "I figured I'd just come along too."

Beau turns to Colson and Sage. "You guys wanna go get ready? We'll leave in a few minutes." Colson looks between us and nods, but I don't miss the smirk he gives me once he turns his back to our guest and moves toward his bedroom.

Alone with Beau in the living room, I move to the kitchen and pour myself a healthy dose of liquid gold from the coffeepot and turn to offer him some, a little squeak escaping my lips when I find Beau standing in front of me, his perfect smile looking down at me as concerned eyes roam my face.

I'm rendered speechless—and motionless—as he lifts his hand to sweep a loose tendril of hair behind my ear, the barely there, touch of his fingertip over my temple sensitizing my skin in the same way it did yesterday at the ranch.

"How much sleep did you get last night, angel?"

*God, why do I like that name so damn much when it comes from him?*

"Um..." I say, a little too spellbound right now to formulate words. Why does he have to be so damn *swoony*?

Beau smiles, two identical dimples on either side of his lips popping out and mesmerizing me further.

"So how about you and me make a deal?"

"Huh," I murmur, still a little lost.

He chuckles, and lord almighty, the deep rumbling laugh reaches right down inside me and warms me to the core. "Angel, you with me?"

I shake my head to clear the haze and nod. "Yes... I mean...no?"

His grin widens. "All right, Molly. Stick with me. I'm going to take the kids back to the ranch, and we're gonna be there all day. While we're gone, you're gonna take yourself back to bed, and you sleep, read—do *whatever* you wanna do as long as the end result is that you're *relaxin'*. I'll have everyone back by supper. Sound good?"

A stunned gasp escapes my lips. A *whole day* to myself. No kids. No work. No *anything*.

"You'd do that?"

Beau dips his chin so his eyes are staring straight into mine. "For you, I'm finding I'll do just about anythin' to see you well rested and letting down that hand you're determined to hold up when it comes to you and me."

"I... I don't know what to say," I whisper, my heart racing along in a staccato beat against my chest.

"You don't gotta say a thing, angel. Except maybe a promise to not do a single thing for the rest of the day."

I nod, my throat threatening to close.

Then I'm frozen in place as he leans in and brushes his lips against my temple. "Good girl."

I stay there as he steps back, probably not realizing how much he's just tilted my world on its axis with his kindness, as he gives me the sexiest grin I've ever seen on a man before he lifts his chin and makes his way to the door.

"Round up, kids. Let's move out."

I'm quickly enveloped in three fleeting hugs as Colson, Sage, and Cody rush past me and out the door to get into Beau's truck. That's when I find myself standing in an empty house with absolutely nothing to do and no one to look after except myself for the next eight or so hours. *What on earth just happened?*

But more than that, why the hell am I still standing in my kitchen when there's a warm bed calling my name and a hot new book to read. *Bliss.*

## 10

## BEAU

"You know what, guys," I start, as I look up at the sun's position in the sky. "It's near on supper time and I reckon y'all have worked hard enough today to earn a treat."

"What kind of treat?" Cody asks immediately, lifting his dirt-smeared face. The teenagers look at me inquisitively, too.

I lean on my shovel and make a show of thinking. "Well, I hear Ellie-Mae was bakin' her famous chocolate torte today. And if I'm not mistaken, I reckon she mentioned somethin' 'bout packin' a basket for y'all to take home. So I was thinkin' that maybe, if you have the energy for it, we can go get your sister and go have a picnic down at the lakeside since the weather is real nice and we've still got hours left of daylight. What do ya reckon?"

Cody's eyes light up. "A day at the ranch *and* a picnic? What is this—Christmas?"

I can't help but chuckle, and both Colson and Sage join in with me. "Guess it's just your lucky day then, hey, Cody?" Colson says, mopping his brow with the hem of his T-shirt.

"And mine," Sage puts in. "If there's chocolate cake, I'm there."

"Good call," I say, tossing my shovel in the back of the Gator. "How 'bout we head back and wash up while Ellie finishes gettin' our picnic together."

"Yeah!" Cody rushes to the Gator and gets in the back.

"Are we ever gonna learn horse ridin'?" Colson asks before he follows suit.

"Eventually. But it's a little hard bein' on horse-back all day when you're a beginner. So we'll ease into that. Maybe I'll see if we can go for a ride next Saturday when y'all come over."

"We get to come back next weekend?" His eyes go almost as bright as Cody's did about the cake. Seems this kid has rancher blood running through him.

"You can come back any time you like. As long as your sister is OK with it and your homework is done."

He nods and I slap him on the back good naturedly. We then both get into the vehicle before I turn us around and zoom back to the ranch house.

Ellie-Mae, god love her, already has the picnic basket packed and ready when we walk in the door. And after we all clean up and I've changed out of my work clothes, we load ourselves into my truck and head back to Molly's.

I've enjoyed having three helpers hanging about this weekend. The way they chatter constantly and tease each other whenever they get a chance reminds me of simpler times when my brothers and I were growing up and driving our dad nuts. Not that I think I'm the dad in this situation, but spending time with this lot gives me a little insight and makes me think that maybe I'd be a decent one...someday.

"Hey guys," Molly says as soon as she opens the door. "How was work?"

"Great!"

"Awesome!"

"Loved it!"

All three kids answer at the same time, rushing past her so they can change out of their stinky clothes. Molly covers her mouth and giggles as she steps aside to let them through. "Gosh, it feels so weird saying that to them."

"I'll bet. Soon it'll become the norm. They'll be grown up and coming and going all the time I guess." I remove my hat and follow behind Molly as she gestures for me to come inside.

"How were they all?"

"Good workers, each and every one of them. Inquisitive too. Like they're really into the whole ranchin' life."

She breathes a sigh of relief. "Funnily enough, they are. Cody is more obvious in his interest, but even Colson, you've given him food for thought, that's for sure."

"Good," I say, a little gruffly, my heart feeling bigger than my chest can hold as I fight against the desire to pull this alluring woman into my arms and kiss you like I've been craving to do for weeks now.

"I'm so happy to hear they weren't any trouble. Next time, I'll have to come along too. It's not fair to lump them all on you when they—"

"I'm gonna stop you right there, angel," I say, holding a hand up. "They *helped* me all day long and made the workday finish a heck of a lot sooner than it would've if it was just me doin' it.

So, I'm grateful for that. And if you're up for it, the kids and I thought we could all go have a picnic together down by the lake. Ellie-Mae made us up a basket, so there's nothin' for you to do but go put on some shoes and get your ass in my truck."

Molly laughs as she looks down at her hoodie and sweatpants. "I think I'll need a little more than a pair of shoes. But yeah, I think taking them on a picnic after working all day is a fitting reward for their efforts. Give me ten minutes and I'll be ready to go."

Giving her a nod, I wait in the living room, watching her go and thinking that I wouldn't half mind going anywhere with her wearing a hoodie and sweats and her hair piled up on her head like that, it's cute. I'm knocked out of my thoughts about Molly when the kids come back to join me and we wait for Molly to finish changing together.

"What's taking so long?" Cody moans, leaning back on the couch dramatically.

"She's probably too busy workin' on that 'makeup but no makeup' look she prides herself on," Sage puts in, earning a giggle from the others.

"All right, now. Give your sister a moment. We did kind of spring this on her," I say, just as Molly appears in the doorway, her hair out and brushed until it shines, and a hint of makeup I'm guessing is that 'no-makeup look' Sage mentioned. *Not that she needs any help in that department, she's beautiful just as she is.* She's wearing a pair of skin-tight jeans, boots, and a pretty blue blouse with little white flowers stitched all over it, and sleeves that fall off her shoulders exposing a stretch of delicate, tanned skin that has me salivating at the sight. *Do not get hard. Do not get hard. Do not get hard.*

"Ready," she chirps, as Colson lets out a low whistle and Sage jumps up to get a closer look at Molly's outfit.

"Is this new?"

"No." Pink brightens Molly's cheeks. "It's been in my wardrobe for years. I'm just never out of work clothes or pajamas, so I don't get the chance to wear half my stuff."

"Oh. Well, it's pretty." Sage smiles and bounces back to the rest of us as Molly's eyes land on mine, an adorable shyness tinging her cheeks. *Don't get hard, Beau. Not now.*

"It's too much, isn't it?"

"No," I say, standing and moving closer to her while making it more than obvious that I'm checking her out approvingly. "I'd say you look like summer itself."

She blushes. "Thanks. It's kind of exciting getting a day off and having somewhere to go for a change. I wanted to mark the occasion."

"Can we goooo?" Cody cuts in. "I'm starrrrving!"

Molly giggles and I offer her my arm, wanting the reassurance of the tingling burn of the Call under my skin to remind me why I need to take this slow and steady. It's a marathon, not a sprint, after all. "Shall we?"

She nods and we all pile back into my truck and get on the road, heading for the local parklands surrounding the lake where there's plenty of space to stretch out and toss around a ball for some fun.

Which is exactly what we do, all of us helping to lay out two big picnic blankets I'd put in the trunk before spreading out Ellie-Mae's delicious smelling food—the chocolate torte, all the fixings for us to make our own sub sandwiches, and fresh homemade lemonade in a big glass bottle. We start eating while Molly asks the kids about their day and Cody regales us with his animated commentary about Miller's cow, Petunia, Jesse's horse, Buster, and Kendra's cat, Spencer, all conspiring against Sawyer throughout the day. The kid is a born storyteller, I'll give him that.

"Colson, did you tell Beau you might be interested in ranchin' as a career path?" Molly says.

"Is that true?" I ask, turning to Colson.

He nods as he takes a big bite out of his salami, ham, and salad sandwich. "Yeah." His eyes drift to his older sister and I don't miss the soft care in his gaze before he turns back to me. "I've been wonderin' for a while what I might wanna do once I graduate, and I've always liked the more physical side of things rather than academic."

I chuckle because he sounds just like me. "Lemme guess, shop and gym are your best subjects? 'Cause they were definitely mine."

"I can take or leave the book stuff, but using my hands to make stuff or *do* stuff gives me a sense of achievement. Like I can *see* the fruit of my labor, I guess."

Nodding, I glance to Molly to see her eyes are a little glassy, but they're happy tears going by the gentle smile caressing her lips. *Stop thinking about her lips, asshole.*

"Well," I say, finishing up my supper and leaning back on my arms. "If you're serious about it, I think there could definitely be a place for you at Eagle Mountain when you're ready."

"*After* college, of course," Molly adds.

"Do they even teach ranching at college?" he asks, his eyes turning to me.

I offer an understanding smile. "No. But there are a lot of things that happen on a ranch that college *can* teach you. Like business, for example. My brother Randy went to college for business, so that's why he's in charge of runnin' things. The rest of us are just the grunts."

"See?" Molly adds. "And college will be such a great experience for you, Cols. I didn't get to stay long, but gosh, I had fun."

Colson may roll his eyes at his sister, but he's also shooting her a grin that's full of respect and love. It's good to see not only Colson, but the other kids too, know how good their sister is and also have the utmost respect for her. With a life of loss like they've had so far, some families would disintegrate under the weight of their grief, but the Roberts family have used it to make themselves closer and stronger than ever.

"What about you, Sage? You had any thought as to what you might wanna do after school?"

"I think…" She shakes her head. "Nah. It's a dumb dream."

Molly bumps Sage with her elbow before shifting closer and wrapping an arm around her sister's shoulders. "C'mon, sis. I know you keep your cards pretty close to your chest. But I really wanna know too."

Sage looks to her sister and nods before returning her eyes to me. "I want to study to be a counselor, one that helps families like ours who lose people important to them and want to stay together." Her voice starts off soft and a little cautious, but there's no missin' the moment she hits her stride and her passion for the vocation shines through. "Like what happens if we didn't have Molly to step in and keep us together? We could've ended up being separated and living in different parts of the state. And I know it's hard, but Molly never lets any of us feel like we're a burden to her either. I'd just like to be as helpful as I can to other kids, other families, who find themselves going through tough times and aren't as lucky as us to have a Molly, or even who live in such a supportive small town like we do."

I have to blink a few times and swallow down hard to get my own emotions under control. Molly doesn't even try to hide the effect of Sage's words as she gasps and envelopes her sister in a big bear hug, burying her face in her neck, Sage rubbing her back with a gentle giggle. "C'mon, Molls. It's not *that* big of a deal."

Molly straightens and looks her sister straight in the eye. "It *is* and I'm so damn proud of the woman you're becoming. You're going to change the world, and I can't wait to have a front-row seat to watch it happen." Sage's eyes widen and she digs her teeth into her lip. There's no hiding the fact that Molly's own words have touched her deeply.

Colson meets my eyes and widens them slightly as if to say, "Chicks, man," which makes me grin.

"Well, *I* want to be an astronaut," Cody announces around a mouthful of food. "Or maybe a cowboy like Beau and Jesse. Or go be a bull rider at the rodeo like Sawyer. Or—"

"Basically, you wanna do anything and everything. Am I right?" Colson says with an amused grin and an arched brow.

"Well, *duh*. Molly always says I can be anything I wanna be."

"Why don't you try bein' a space cowboy?" Colson suggests.

Cody's eyes bug out. "Is that an option?"

"Not yet," Molly says with a laugh. "But maybe someday. When we're all living in spaceships."

"Aw, nuts. That sounded fun." Cody folds his arms and pouts.

"*Well*," I say, eying up the chocolate dessert. "Now that we all know our future, we have a very important decision to make."

Molly tilts her head to the side and scrunches her little button nose up, just that one look making my cock take notice. "What's that?"

"Football or torte?"

"Football!" all three kids and Molly reply in unison before dissolving into laughter.

"The tribe has spoken," Molly says, her eyes never leaving mine as I stand and hold out my hands to help her to her feet. The warmth that courses through me when she slides her hands into mine is enough to melt the polar ice caps if need be. Global warming is already something we had to worry about, and I've got to wonder if this need burning inside me to make this woman mine is going to contribute to the situation. Seems it continues to blaze hotter and brighter the more I see of her. I'm getting more and more certain that what's happening here is the Call. *What else could it be?*

Molly's eyes flash with surprise as I pull her up, squeezing her fingers when she's standing in front of me, both to check that she's steady but also to stop myself from what I really wanna do which is pull her hard up against me and touch my lips to hers.

"Hey, Beau. Can I be on *your* team? It can be the biggest and the smallest versus Sage, Cols, and Molly," Cody asks, sidling up beside me.

"Sure thing, bud," I say, leaning down a bit. "But we need something to play for. What do you say about the winners getting the first pieces of cake?"

"Yesssss!" he says, jumping up and down. "Right. C'mon, Beau. Time for us to kick some butt."

"Yes, sir,"

"Well then, ladies," I say, including Colson in that with a knowing smirk. "Time to see what you're made of." I wink at Molly, loving the spark of fire in her eyes and the determination in her features.

"Just you wait, Beau Barnes. You should never underestimate the underdog. You never quite know when they'll pop up and surprise you," she says.

"Underestimating you, Angel, is something I'll never do."

"I CAN'T BELIEVE we beat you guys," Cody says, hopping out of my truck the minute I put it in park. "It was two on three, you guys totally should've won." The kid has been buzzing ever since he and I were declared the winners and I graciously—OK, I would've done it anyway—let him cut the first piece of torte and claim his prize.

"Maybe we *let* you win," Colson teases, following behind the youngest Roberts member.

"Yeah right. There's no way you'd *let* us win. Right, Sage?" Cody turns around and walks backward up the stairs to the porch, his eyes narrowed on his sister.

"Nah. We're all about winning in this family. You won, fair and square, kiddo."

"Yesssss," he hisses, disappearing into the house, his loud footsteps thudding down the hallway as the kids file inside, Colson sneaking me a knowing smirk before closing the door to leave Molly and me alone on the porch. *The kid is definitely not missin' what's going on here.*

She wrings her hands in front of her before she lifts her eyes to mine. "Thank you for today, I think it might just be the most relaxing day I've had in a long time. We'll have to add it to the list of things I have to repay you for." She reaches out and places her hand on my arm, the small smile playing at her lips making my heart skip a beat and my blood pump harder in my veins. *This woman has no idea what she does to me.*

"It was no trouble," I reply roughly, unable to hide the effect she's having on me.

She flexes her fingers against my skin and I swear I feel the jolt straight down into my soul.

"It is, and it was also very thoughtful."

"You don't have to repay me, though. Just knowing you had a good day is all the thanks I need. Friends don't owe friends for every little thing." Her lashes flutter shut, a soft sigh escaping her lips as she pulls her hand away. I feel the loss immediately.

*God, she's beautiful.*

Cody's voice calling out to her breaks me out of the moment, Molly's gorgeous hazel eyes opening to meet mine. "I better go see what he wants," she whispers.

"Yeah…"

Then, as if my body moves of its own volition, I step forward, dip my head and brush my lips against the corner of her mouth, teasing myself more than fulfilling the gnawing need building inside me to kiss her the way I'm desperate to kiss her. I could swear I feel her body sway toward mine, and hear a soft moan of want escaping her lips.

"I'll see you soon, angel," I breathe, not missing the hitch in her breath as I shift back and grin down at her flushed expression as I start toward the steps.

"Next Saturday?" she asks, her voice full of hope as I reach the bottom.

This time, there's no stopping the grin covering my lips as I turn around and shoot her a grin. "As far as I'm concerned, angel. Next weekend can't come soon enough."

## 11

## MOLLY

It's Friday night, but this time I'm not working. And despite working at the Vet Clinic this morning and helping Mrs. Murphy with some gardening this afternoon, the chores never do themselves, even after my many years of hoping that they will. So with Cody in bed and the older two in their rooms doing whatever it is that teenagers do, I've parked myself on the couch, poured myself a glass of wine, and with the television on in the background, I'm folding the clean laundry that's built up during the week.

Despite working all hours of the day and night—well, not that many, but that's how it seems sometimes—I do try to keep an organized and ordered house. This means I've had to become a multitasker. Thankfully, it's something I've now perfected into a fine art.

But even with so many things going on in my life, I can't stop my brain from drifting back to Beau and the butterflies in my stomach about seeing him again tomorrow. It's crazy how often I've found myself thinking about the man this week, and about last Sunday at the picnic and the cheek kiss on the doorstep when he dropped the kids off.

The kiss though, I don't even know *why* I'm so fixated on it. It wasn't even a *kiss* kiss, yet it was so much more than the kiss on the temple he'd given me when he picked the kids up that morning. It was so close to my mouth that I could feel his warm breath fan over my skin. But more than that, my heart almost leaped out of my chest when his lips brushed ever so lightly against my cheek. I had to tense every single muscle in my body to stop from turning my head just that little bit so that he *did* kiss me. Like my soul, my brain, my *everything* was aching to feel his lips on mine. I've *never* felt that kind of intense draw before. And the way Beau's eyes darkened, and his breath caught when he pulled away and met my gaze, will forever be burned into my psyche. At that moment I knew... I *knew* that he wanted me. *I knew I wanted him too...*

And now I'm wondering whether it's too late to change my mind? Like, 'Hey, sorry I said I didn't want to date anyone right now, but I think... I know... I mean, maybe... I might be rethinking my stance on the matter..." *Yeah, talk about hot and cold, Molly!*

I lean forward and grab my wine glass, lifting it to my mouth and taking a big gulp just as my phone starts vibrating on the coffee table, Kendra's name flashing on the screen.

Picking it up, I bring it to my ear. "Hey, Kendie," I say, abandoning the laundry and cradling my drink while leaning back into the sofa.

"Hey, Molls. How are you doing?"

"I'm good. Tired after weeding Mrs. Murphy's garden this afternoon, but she kept me fed with savory muffins and iced tea. We even ended the day with a small tipple of port she keeps stashed away for special occasions."

Kendra laughs. "She's a character, that one. I'll bet her malamute, Doug, loved the cuddles you gave him too."

"Doesn't he always? I'm his favorite human other than his mama."

"Well, he sure doesn't like me after I had to give him his booster shot last week."

"To be fair," I say with a smile, "I'm not sure *I* would even like you much if you gave me jabs in my rump either."

"Too true." She chuckles. "So I was wondering if you were coming out to the ranch tomorrow?"

My brows furrow as I frown at the TV. "Sure am. Why's that?"

"No reason." But there's something funny in her voice that piques my curiosity.

"Oh no. There's *definitely* a reason. Why's that, Kendie?"

"'Cause Beau got Jesse and Sawyer helping to get enough horses ready for all of us to go for a ride. And since that *never* happens—well not without good reason—I thought I'd check in with you."

"You're not making any sense, Kendra."

"I'm just..." The call falls silent, but I swear I can hear her mind working overtime. Otherwise, it's mine, which is *also* a possibility. "What do you think about Beau these days?"

"Um... that's a weird question."

She sighs. "Well, not really. I mean, you've gone from saying you're not dating anyone, and then all week at work I keep catching you day-dreaming and staring off into space with a cute little grin on your face, *and* the guys *might* have been teasing Beau about how they've never seen him do so much and spend so much time with a woman before." *Now that is interesting.*

"These days....we're friends. That's all we can be," I say, even though I'm not dumb enough to lie to myself that I'm seriously reconsidering my stance on that subject, especially after the way my body reacted to the almost lip kiss last weekend.

"But what if—" She cuts herself off.

"What if *what*, Kendie?"

"What if Beau wants to be more than friends? What *if* you and Beau came into each other's lives at this time for a reason?"

I snort. I can't help it. "The Call and the Mountain Spirit have totally made you sappy, haven't they?"

"Maybe..." she says in a singsong voice. "But it still begs the question... Would it be *so* bad if you kept an open mind when it comes to you and Beau? I mean, as far as good men go, you can't get much better than Beau Barnes."

"Don't let your cowboy hear you say that."

"I'm right here beside her, and don't worry, I'll make her pay for saying my brother is a better man than me," Jesse says into the phone. Kendra gasps, and there's a rustling sound in my ear.

"Ignore him. I am," she says with a giggle.

"Heard that too, doc. Just you wait till you're off the phone. I'll show you how *good* I can be," he growls, and now I'm laughing along with her.

"I better let you go so your *cowboy* can give you the good stuff."

"OK, but before you do, can I say something and you have to promise you'll think about it before tomorrow?"

Since I have a feeling I'm gonna need it, I take another sip of my wine before replying. "All right, Kendie. Hit me with your sage advice."

"This is all I'm gonna say. As your person, your bestie, and your all-around favorite human who *isn't* related to you, I just want you to think about this. Taking time for yourself doesn't mean you're giving the kids any less. If anything, you're giving them more because there's more of you left to give." I open my mouth to reply, but she keeps going. "And what I mean by that is, you're allowed to look after the kids and work your three jobs, *but* you *can* also have a life too."

"And by that, you mean a love life, don't ya?"

"I'm not gonna say anything else. I just want you to think about it. OK?"

"OK, Kendie. I'll take it on board. Satisfied now?"

"No, but she will be in a minute!" Jesse calls out, and a startled laugh bubbles out of me.

"Now *that* is more than I needed to know. Have a good night, you two. I'll see you tomorrow."

"I'll bring the cowboy coffee!"

"Deal. Bye, bestie."

"Right back at ya, Molls," she says before the call ends.

Then I look down at the three baskets of laundry still left to go through, take another sip from my wineglass, and focus on the job at hand, trying *not* to think about Kendra's suggestion.

Closing down the house for the night, a warm, mellow feeling settles deep in my belly. But alongside it is also a tinge of sadness. Maybe not sadness as such, more melancholy. Because it's times like these, late at night, when the kids are in bed and I finally get time just to *be*, I'm more aware of the consequences of my life choices— especially the one where I dedicate my life to raising the kids and *not* to indulging my romantic heart. I've imagined many times what it would be like to have a partner here with me to share the load, to spend time with on these quiet nights, just cuddling on the couch, talking about our day and the week ahead, organizing who's doing what, who's picking up who and when, and the like. Just someone to *be* with, other than myself. But then I've always discounted that because, seriously, who could ever *want* to take on what I deal with? It's a lot. So I've never let the idea become more than a flight of fancy.

Don't get me wrong, I *love* the life I have with my brothers and sister, and I wouldn't want it any other way—and neither would my father. But in the quiet of night, knowing I should try to get some sleep ahead of yet another busy week of wall-to-wall shifts at the vet clinic, the Lair, and a list longer than my arm of errands to run for Kinleyville residents, I feel the voids in my life more than never.

Then I remember Kendra's words. As hard as I've tried, I haven't been able to *stop* thinking about them since her phone call.

*Taking time for yourself doesn't mean you're giving the kids any less. If anything, you're giving them more because there's more of you left to give*

I didn't get it then, but letting it ruminate while I folded the never ending laundry pile, I'm starting to wonder if closing myself off to the *possibility* of something with a kind, gentle, generous man like Beau Barnes might just be the dumbest decision I've ever made.

Something I keep coming back to is that everything Beau does seems so in tune with what I need in the moment. I'm starting to wonder if he's a mind reader... or even a *mood* reader. He's so cool, calm, and collected, and watching him interact with the kids leaves me in awe every single time. He's so patient with them, and he seems to be able to relate to each of them in his own way. With Cody, he's interesting and attentive. With Sage, he's caring and seems to realize when she's in her own head and just needs to be left to her own devices. And with Colson, it's like he's taken him under his wing, and is now focused on cultivating my brother's interest in ranching. For that, I don't think I'll ever be able to repay him.

And the more time I spend around him, the more understanding he is of my determination to do this on my own without handouts. Despite our age difference, he just...*gets me.* So with each passing moment, I'm starting to so easily see Beau slotting into our lives—into *my* life.

*Whoa there, Molly. Slow down.* He's just being a good friend... right? It's not like he's waiting for me to give him the go-ahead so he can drop down on bended knee.

Laughing to myself, I shake my head. The fact I'm thinking about that could be a sign that I need to take Kendra's words to heart. There's nothing that says a girl can't change her mind in matters of the heart. And there's no harm in *considering* opening myself up to Beau and seeing where the cards fall, either.

And if Kendra and her husband, Jesse, are anything to go by, there are far worse things in life than falling in love with a cowboy. Especially one as good and as kind as Beau...

With that in mind, I change into my pajamas and slip into bed, snuggling down and grabbing my Aster book, losing myself in the story of a sexy, charming cowboy who finds his soulmate on a ranch. All the while, I'm hoping Aster's words will inspire some vivid dreams about the irresistible, charming, and definitely sexy Beau Barnes. You know, I might just open my heart up to him after all...

"There's a cat on the back of this horse," Cody says, giggling as we meander along the well-worn path. "How'd Spencer even get here?"

I glance back to see Spencer cleaning his paws while he sits on Buster's rump, balancing like he was born there. "He must've been hidin' in the saddlebags. He does that sometimes."

"I like it!" Cody declares.

"Ain't never seen a cat ridin' horseback before," Sage says, joining in the laughter.

"Reckon he needs a tiny hat and vest if he's gonna look the part," Molly adds. Colson just rolls his eyes and smiles, possibly too mature in this moment to join in the fun. He's taking this ranching thing seriously. However, I'm not sure how serious he is about going to college like Molly wants. I'm not one to stick my nose into another's affairs, but I will strongly encourage them to talk it out whenever the opportunity arises. Life's too short to fill it with obligation.

"Tell Ellie-Mae that. She'll have something stitched up in no time," I say with a smile.

"I think I'd like to see that," Colson says.

"Just you wait then. Ellie loves anything to do with whimsy."

Chatter about Spencer dressed as a cowboy continues while we head back to the ranch. We've just spent a few hours driving the cows into the new paddock before stopping for lunch at a waterfall and heated spring on the edge of our lands, dubbed Paradise Springs for its year-round warmth. Even in the dead of winter you can go out there and warm up in the waters. Kendra assures us there's some magic there, and I'm inclined to agree. In a place like that—sitting, eating, and talking like an actual family—well, anything feels possible.

When we get to the barn, I show the kids how to unsaddle the horses and brush them down before giving them their feed and leading everyone back to the main house to wash up.

"I've baked a pie for y'all to take home with you," Ellie-Mae says as we pass through. "It's apple and salmonberry, and I have to admit, it's delicious. We had a bumper harvest this year."

"You can berry pick here, too?" Sage gasps.

"Why sure we can. We grow just about everythin' we need here, petal. Next time you're here, I'll take you out to our little greenhouse and show you around. You can pick whatever you like to take back home with you."

"Really?" Sage looks like a kid in a candy store.

"Of course."

Which is when Molly's pride kicks in. "Oh no, El-lie-Mae. You're already giving us so much. We couldn't take your produce too," she says.

But in true Ellie-Mae fashion, she doesn't miss a beat or take no for an answer. "So you'd rather it all go rotten on the ground? There's more than we can possibly eat ourselves in there, so if you don't take it, it'll be a waste."

"Oh, I'm sorry. I didn't realize," Molly says. "Of course we'll help you make use of it." *Well played, Ellie.*

"Excellent," Ellie-Mae says. "And you'll help me by taking this extra pie too. I'm always makin' too much, and half the time these scraps end up in the pig trough. Such a waste." She pouts, making Molly laugh.

"Now I know you're tellin' fibs, because I've seen those brothers of yours eat, and there ain't a shred of chicken left on any of those wings."

Ellie grins and thrusts the pie forward. "You still have to take the pie."

"OK. I will," Molly concedes. "But only if it'll help you."

I chuckle to myself over the exchange as I walk Molly and the kids out to their truck so Molly can get back home in time to get ready for her shift at the Lair. After a long day working together out in the sun, the kids have all gotten the hang of riding the horses, and Molly, it seems, already knew how. She says that she couldn't be besties with Kendra and not know how to ride, which seems pretty reasonable to me.

"Thanks again for today. What time do you want to pick the kids up tomorrow?" Molly says, turning to me once everyone is loaded into the truck. It's one of the many moments today that she's lifted her eyes to mine and I've witnessed a blush bloom across those pretty cheeks of hers. Without even thinking, my hand lifts to cradle her cheek and I brush my thumb over her soft skin.

"I'll come by after breakfast. But only if you promise that tomorrow will be your day of rest."

She leans into my touch and her eyes flutter closed for the brief moment we're connected. I lower my hand and place it on the top of her open car door.

"How come you keep insistin' I take a day off, but you seem to work from sunup to sundown, seven days a week?"

"Because I don't consider this work," I say with a grin. "I consider this ranch an extension of me, so every single thing I do counts as self-care."

She laughs a little as she pulls her bottom lip between her teeth. *Lord, do I wanna suck that thing free.*

"There's definitely something about this place. I'll give you that."

"Like what?"

She looks around for a moment thoughtfully. "Like it rejuvenates your spirit somehow."

"Yeah?"

"Yeah. Even though I've been here all day, I don't even feel like I was workin'. So I guess what you're sayin' makes sense."

"I'm glad we could come to an agreement."

"Oh, I think you'll find we agree on a lot of things, Beau Barnes."

I lift my brow in question. "Such as?"

"That the Lair makes the best wings for miles."

"Yeah."

"And that bein' outside is way better than bein' indoors."

"Also true."

"That family means everything."

"Yes."

"And you're probably the most amazin' and understandin' man I think I've ever known."

A small smile tugs at my lips as I move back a little. "Amazin' and understandin', huh? I'll have to take your word on that one."

"It's true. I know you don't like me saying I owe you anything, but I do feel I owe you a debt of gratitude. You're changin' my life here."

"For the better, I hope."

She smiles, then presses up on her toes and kisses the underside of my jaw. "Definitely."

And with that, she hops into her truck and heads off, while I'm just stuck standing here trying to decipher exactly what just happened. Molly kissed me. Not the other way around. Sure, it was just a peck, but that has to mean something, right?

As she drives off the ranch, I lift my hand and wave before lowering it to the space where her kiss landed once she's out of sight. It has to mean something, and I won't let nothin' or no one tell me otherwise.

"How'd romancin' Molly go today?" Sawyer asks as I meet everyone around the fire pit after the sun has gone down. It's close to midnight, and we should have all been in bed long ago. But summer is for taking advantage of the daylight, so we tend to rise early and bed down late. No one here's complaining.

"I wanna hear this one," Jesse says, handing me a bottle of beer as I sit beside him. "Kendra's been chompin' at the bit waitin' for somethin' to happen between you two."

"Why's Kendra so interested?" Randy puts in. "Does she know somethin' we don't?"

Jesse grins then mimes zipping his lips, locking it, and throwing away the key. Miller barks out a laugh.

"It's like Gandalf all over again. The seer we had on Bear used to talk in riddles, and it drove us all nuts. But once your Call is complete, you're actually kinda glad they didn't tell you everything. I kinda reckon it'd take some of the magic away from it."

"From what Kendra says, the biggest rule about bein' a seer is knowin' and not sharin'. Just guidin'. Y'all have to muddle your way through it the way me and Miller did with doc and Ellie."

"True that," Miller says, nodding sagely.

I twist the cap off my beer and take a thirsty drink while I ponder their words. "Are we even sure this *is* the Call? I mean, Molly's comin' 'round, but I don't think she's as into me as I am her. When I'm with her, it's like I'm tryin' real hard to get close but not startle her and cause her to run away."

"So she's a deer?" Randy suggests, causing a ripple of laughter to roll around the pit.

"Not a deer. Just...tapped out. Her shoulders are broad, but they're overloaded. Like she's scared takin' anythin' else on would tip her balance too far."

"I always thought she had slender shoulders," Sawyer muses.

"It's a sayin' nitwit," Randy says with a laugh. "Means she has a lot going on and can't handle much more."

"Ohhhh." Sawyer tips his head back and slowly nods. Sometimes I think he might've hit his head a few too many times when getting thrown off those bulls.

"And she does," I continue on from Randy. "So I'm just tryin' to help lessen that weight a little. She takes' everythin' on for everyone else, and I'm tryin' to be that someone she needs in her corner."

"She needs someone? Or do you just need to *be* that someone?" Randy asks. "There's a difference."

I flick the rim of my bottle with the edge of my thumbnail. "Dunno. Both, maybe? I just feel like this is the right thing for me to do."

"Sounds like the Call to me," Jesse says, tapping the side of my boot with the toe of his.

"Doin' stuff for a girl when it seems hopeless, but you just gotta do it anyway?" Miller nods. "That's the Call, all right."

"How can you be so sure?" I ask. "I mean, I might just be infatuated with some young filly I shouldn't even be thinkin' about the way I do."

Sawyer leans back and chuckles. "That's my entire weekend."

"I can't wait until the Call comes for you, brother," Randy says. "She's gonna make you work so hard for it, and you won't know what the hell hit you."

"Who's the seer now?" Miller teases as he tips his bottle back and drains it.

"Seems like sweet justice to me," Randy says, and we all nod and chuckle in agreement while Sawyer rolls his eyes.

"No Call is comin' this way. I'm gonna be a bachelor till I die. This land and the rodeo, that's all I'll ever need."

"OK," Miller says. "Well, when you meet a girl and your heart starts pounding in your chest—"

"And your skin gets so hot it's like you're on fire," Jesse adds before Miller jumps back in.

"And every time you're near, there's an electrical current in the air, and all you can do is think about how desperately you wanna touch her."

Jesse nods. "And then when you do touch her, it's not enough. You need more, more—"

"More. Until you're so crazy from fightin' it, you collide and *boom*." Miller claps his hands together, the sound cutting through the still night air. "Nothing will ever be right without them."

"That's the Call," Jesse says, tapping the neck of his bottle against mine. "And I know for a fact y'all are gonna experience it. And want it or not" —his eyes fall on Sawyer—"you're gonna answer."

Sawyer shrugs and chugs the rest of his beer while I just stare down at my hands, running through the list Miller and Jesse rattled off and realizing that most of it—well, the part before the boom—is already happening to me. *Well, fuck.*

"You OK there, Beau?" Randy asks across the flames.

I look up and lock eyes with him, my heart hammering as the realization hits. "I think I'm hearing the Call."

## 13

## MOLLY

J ust after lunchtime on Tuesday, after a full-on morning of back-to-back appointments, Kendra came out of her consultation room at the Vet clinic and asked if I wanted to go have lunch with her at the diner. Which is how I find myself sitting in a window booth at Betty's with an almost empty coffee mug and a half-eaten plate of the diner's famous Sloppy Joe casserole.

"So...you doing OK? Outside of everyday life?" she asks curiously as Beatrice, the diner's owner, swings past and tops up our coffee cups.

I grin against the mug as I meet her eyes, tilting my head and studying her. "I'm good. A hell of a lot better after having two Sundays in a row off. That Beau really is as good-hearted as you say he is, that's for sure."

She leans her elbows onto the table. "Now tell me about that. Beau keeps a lot to himself at the best of times, but he didn't say much about it, especially to me. All he did say was that the kids were spending the day at the ranch and you were having a day to yourself. Did you *ask* him to do that? 'Cause honey, you know Jesse and I will take Cody off your hands whenever you want."

My expression goes soft as I reach over and cover her hand with mine, giving it a gentle squeeze before pulling back and cradling my mug. "I know, and if I ever get caught short, I'll totally take you guys up on that. But Beau didn't exactly give me a choice."

Kendra's brows narrow. "What do you mean?"

"The first time, he came to pick up Colson, and Cody and Sage wanted to go too. Then he pretty much insisted I stay home, go back to bed and have a day off from life. Then he did it again this weekend. I feel like a new woman."

Her eyes widen before her lips slowly curl up into a smirk. "Knew that man had a gooey side."

My head jerks back. "Um... we're talking about Beau. You know, your brother-in-law? The kind, gentle, sweet man who looks better in a pair of jeans than your husband."

Her mouth twitches. "No one looks better than my man does in a pair of jeans."

"Except Beau, of course."

"Those cowboys sure know how to wear their Levis."

"That, they do," I say, before I take a deep breath, my brain running over all the reasons why I *shouldn't* be thinking about being with Beau in denim and finding that the cons list has been growing more and more empty the more time I spend with the wonderful man. Maybe I'm allowed to gush about the man a little? That's what besties do, right?

"He's quite remarkable," I continue. "He's so good with the kids, all three of them, and I can tell they love spending time at the ranch and learning about the animals and working the land. And it doesn't matter how many questions they ask him, he gives them his full attention and answers everything they want to know. Like when we went horse riding with everyone yesterday. You saw him, right? He was so attentive and was watching the four of us like a hawk. You definitely wouldn't think he lives and works around men all day, every day."

"Don't forget about Ellie-Mae. She's the mother hen of the ranch house. She's been keeping all those guys in check for years now."

"Well, I'll have to commend her on a job well done next time I see her."

Kendra's eyes twinkle with amusement as a wicked grin transforms her features. "If I didn't know better, I'd say you have a big ol' crush on Beau Barnes."

"What?" I whisper, my body going still. "No. I just mean he's a nice guy. Caring, responsible, thoughtful."

"And you're *totally* swooning right now. Quick, Molly. You better be careful, that romance-loving heart of yours is showing." Kendra laughs and gives me a wink.

I shake my head, my cheeks heating as I wave her off before stuffing another mouthful of casserole in my mouth, mainly to stop myself from talking.

Thankfully, she lets it go and we fall into a comfortable silence while finishing our lunch, eventually shifting into small talk about the clinic and Kendra updating me on the latest news about her growing horse rescue center.

"Hey. Do you know what kind of things Beau likes? I was thinking of getting him a little something to say thank you from me and the kids."

"You wanna buy him a gift?" she asks, waggling her eyebrows. "You sound smitten, you know that, right?"

I gasp. "What? No. I just want to repay him for his kindness. I'd thought about something from the bookshop, but then I don't even know if he reads."

"If he gets the chance to read, it's probably farm machinery repair manuals or farming magazines."

"We'll that option is out then." I tap my chin, wracking my brain for ideas. "What about a new hat? Surely a rancher can never have enough hats."

She shakes her head. "Oh no. A rancher picks his own hats. It's their god-given right, apparently. And it has to be the perfect fit. It takes time and research apparently," she says with an exaggerated roll of her eyes.

"All right then. You learn something new every day." I stop and think. "I know. What about a dinner voucher? Or a nice bottle of bourbon? Better still, a bottle of bourbon *and* dinner with you."

"What? No." I move my head side to side. "That wouldn't be a good idea, Kendie." Although now I'm thinking about what it *would* be like to go to dinner with him. Like a date. Where I'd dress up intending to render him speechless, and he'd wear a nice shirt over that big chest of his, the sleeves rolled up to the elbows giving me a little glimpse of his tattoos I've only seen a teasing glance of. I wonder if he'd pull out my chair and compliment me? Maybe we'd flirt a little during the meal, the conversation flowing easily over good food and a perfectly matched wine he'd choose before we'd end the night with a chaste kiss on my doorstep. "Do you think he sees me as too young for him?"

"No," Kendra replies right away. "I think he sees you just as you are. And he doesn't want a gift from you, he just wants *you*."

"Hmm." I press my lips together and all of a sudden images of us walking hand in hand along a moonlit street light up my brain.

"Molly, I love you, and usually I'd let you get away with doing a terrible job at hiding the fact you think Beau is the best Barnes brother. But I'm thinking there's one thing you *haven't* considered yet when it comes to you and my brother-in-law, and I don't just mean what I told you to think about last week on the phone."

Now she's got my attention. "OK, wise one. What is that?"

"First, humor me for a moment. Have you been feeling a little *off* lately?"

I rub my chin and realize I have been a bit off my game, especially those weird tingles and aches in my chest. *Maybe I should make an appointment with the doctor or something?*

Looking over at her, I'm met with a wry grin. She looks like a cat that got the cream. "You have, right? And what about your heart, has it been beating a little strangely?"

My eyes bug out of my head as I gasp. "How do you know that?"

"And does it sometimes feel like you've stuck a fork into a power outlet? You know, like the hairs standing up on your arms and your body feeling—"

"Electrified?" I whisper, earning myself a nod.

"What's going on, Kendie?"

She holds her hand up. "One last thing." She crooks her finger, urging me to come in close as she does the same. "Do you ever feel... No, it's more than just a feeling. Do you ever *sense* when Beau is close? Like your body and soul lets you know he's near?" *There's no way in hell she should know any of this.* I sit back, my brows lifting sky high, my eyes as wide as saucers, and my mouth dropped open like I'm a Venus flytrap waiting for my next meal.

"Kendra, you're starting to freak me out."

She shakes her head and shoots me a gentle smile. "Sorry, honey. That's not my intention. But you *have* just confirmed my thoughts."

"Which are?"

"Do you remember a few months ago when you and I sat at this very table and I told you how Jesse came back from Bear Mountain and told me I was his soulmate and that a Mountain Spirit called me to the ranch for him?"

I fight to swallow down my mouthful and nod, urging her to go on.

"Right. And how he and I were destined to be together?"

"Yeah... you also told me you could see the future in your dreams and you were a... what was it again?"

"A seer. Eagle Mountain's Seer."

"Yeah, that. I remember. What has that got to do with you asking about the weird things I've been experiencing lately?" Maybe I need more Sundays without kids or work. I'm feeling like there are dots I should be connecting right now and I'm not.

She levels me with a pointed stare, neither one of us saying anything as silence stretches between us. My heart thumping against my sternum like

I've been running *up* a damn mountain, not talking about a mystical being that's supposedly handpicking soulmates for men who live, work, and protect the land— *Oh shit.*

My mouth is suddenly as dry as the Great Kobuk Sand Dunes, and there's no way I can speak right now, because surely my best friend, my boss, my *person* is not actually telling me that not only can she see the future, but that I'm... that Beau is...

"You've read the books, Molls. You *know* what I'm saying... You *know*."

Oh. My. God. There's no way I could be...

"Ever wonder why Beau came into your life?"

"Because of you and Jesse."

She sighs. "That's how you met him. I'm saying, that night the kids were hitchhiking, Beau told us to go ahead. Now I don't know exactly why he did that, because we usually all go to and from the Lair together. But that night, he'd also decided to take his truck instead of piling in with everyone else, and then he *chose* to go the long way home near the lake. And just *happened* to come across the kids." She pauses as if letting those coincidences I'd never considered before sink in. "And that night, is that when the heart palpitations started? And the tingling in your skin? And the inability to think about anything but him?"

No. It can't be true. That would mean that the Call is *real* and there's no way that could be true.

My stance is wavering, but I'm not ready to admit that yet. "That doesn't mean he's my..." I can't even say it, scared of what it might mean if I do.

"You have to say it, Molls. I can't confirm it unless you draw the conclusion yourself."

My eyes lock with hers as my heart thunders in my ears. "He's my soulmate," I whisper, and a big smile spreads across my friend's face as she nods.

"Yes, Molly. According to the mountain lore and the visions in my dreams, you and Beau are meant to be together. And it may come as a shock to you, but this is a good thing, honey." She reaches out and covers my trembling hands with hers. "I see good things on the horizon for you."

I stare at her, my lips opening and closing as her words sink in. "Whoa."

Of *course* I know about the Call. Kendra told me bits and pieces about it when she and Jesse were working toward being together and staying together. And I've read Aster Hollingsworth's stories about a spirit calling soulmates to be with the mountain man protectors of the land. But that's fiction. What Kendra is telling me is that the lines between fiction and reality are blurred... like crisscrossing all over the page, blurred. And that's something that'll take a bit of time—and a bottle of wine—to sink in and get used to.

Because if what Kendra says is true, Beau and I are destined to be together regardless of the obstacles. And all this time I've been closing myself off to the *possibility* of being with Beau. I've been wasting precious time with my *one true love*.

"What do you need, Molly? A day off, meditation, a girls' night with takeout, trashy TV, and tequila?"

I lift my eyes to meet Kendra's concerned gaze, a slow-growing smile covers my face. Because *this* is the last sign I needed to show myself that I can do everything for the kids *and* maybe... just maybe... have a life for myself too.

Suddenly, I don't feel like I need any more time to let this sink in. All I need is to step into my own, personalized romance novel and walk my path.

"I think I need to see Beau."

## 14

## BEAU

"Oh, howdy, partner," Ellie says as she approaches me while I'm working stacking pallets in the supply store. "I've heard some whisperings that you might be hearin' the Call. Is that true?"

I set the bag of feed on top of the new pallet before I dust off my hands and turn my attention fully to her. We all take turns with the day-to-day workload at the supply store the same way we do on the ranch. I'm only here a few afternoons a week, but I like it because it helps break up the monotony of always being on the ranch. Not that the work is massively different. It still involves a lot of lifting and sweating it out just the same. Like right now as I transfer bags of feed from an older pallet to a new pallet that I've just dragged out onto the main floor.

"The firepit is supposed to be a sacred man space," I tease, giving her a smirk as she rolls her eyes. "Might have to give Miller an earful for givin' into pillow talk."

Her mouth falls open as she gasps and slaps me playfully on the chest. "The hell it is, it's a *family* space. But for your information, it wasn't Miller who told me at all. It was Randy. He told me this morning while I was brewing up *your* coffee in the kitchen. And I think I have a right to know if my big brother is on the path to his One."

"Path? This feels a lot like anxiety to me," I say with a grunt as another bag hits the pallet.

"Anxiety?" Ellie May pulls her head back and frowns. "How can fallin' in love with your soul-mate feel like *anxiety*?"

I pick up another bag of feed and shift it. "Because my guts are all twisted up and I don't know where I stand with her on any given day. I mean, it feels like we're getting closer, but things are very chaste right now. What's happening, or supposed to happen between us, isn't going *anywhere* unless she chooses it, you know?"

"Yeah. I get that. Do you *want* it to go somewhere?"

"Of course, I do. I think she's smart, sweet, beautiful, and tenacious."

"Fine ways to describe a lady."

"But I also think she's incredibly stubborn and prideful. So it feels like it's more of an endurance race than a sprint to the finish at this point."

"A labor of love, huh?" Ellie-Mae says, with a far-away look in her eyes. The soft romance in her expression makes me smile. It's the same wistful look I've caught on Molly's face a few times when I've done something nice for her.

"I guess you can call it that," I say, continuing to work. "I mean, that's the end goal, right?" I pick up the last bag of feed and drop it on top of the new pile before I lift the old pallet onto its side and walk it over to the stack we have leaned up against the wall.

"What do you think is standing in the way besides Molly's pride and stubbornness?" she asks as follows me.

"I don't know. I suppose it's time. The poor girl is working three jobs to keep them all afloat. Plus, she's runnin' kids around to sporting matches and extracurriculars and whatnot during her time off, so I guess what we need is time to be together, time so she can relax. "

Ellie claps her hands together and smiles. "Excellent."

My brow goes up. "Excellent?"

"Yes! Because I have a solution to that problem. And she'll be getting here any minute now."

"Ellie-Mae Long. You didn't give that girl another job, did you?"

She giggles and nods her blonde head. "I did. But this is replacing all those odd jobs she was doin' 'round town for a pittance. So, I've promised her a steady gig on Tuesday and Thursday afternoon. So, she'll be here the same days you are, and it all fits around her schedule at the vet clinic and the kids. So, this is a win-win."

I grin. I love this woman. A man couldn't ask for a better sister, related by blood or by choice. "In that case, I'll take it. And thank you."

"Anythin' for my favorite brother," she says with a wink, and I laugh because she calls all of us her favorite when the others aren't around.

"Lucky you're my favorite sister too."

"I'm your *only* sister."

"And a wonderful one at that," I say as I envelop her in a hug.

"I just wanna see y'all happy, Beau. You Barnes men have done so much for me, so I really wanna see you experience the same kind of joy I have in my life with Miller and Whitney. The Mountain really does know what She's doin' when she chooses your mate."

"I hope so," I say just as I release her and Miller walks in.

"Hey, what are you doing manhandling my wife?" he teases, approaching us with a cheeky grin on his face. "That's my job."

Ellie Mae squeals as Miller wraps his arms around her waist, then dips her backward and kisses her roughly. I avert my eyes slightly, but I can't help but smile at their display of affection. Because that right there, it's what I want with Molly. And as much as I understand that this is a marathon, I kind of wish we could do a *little* sprinting.

## 15

## MOLLY

The first thing I hear when I enter the Kinleyville Feed and Supply store is giggling, followed by the sounds of amused voices. Seeking them out, I find exactly who I hoped for—Beau—standing with Ellie-Mae and Miller. And just like Kendra mentioned when we were at the diner for lunch yesterday, I *feel* Beau before I even see him. *Thump. Thump. Thump.*

"Hey," I say to get their attention. "Molly Roberts, reporting for duty." I give them a slight salute as I smile their way, enjoying the way Beau's warm eyes move over me. He's the primary reason I accepted this position when Ellie-Mae came into the vet clinic to offer it to me today. I don't know what it was, but I had this deep-seated feeling that coming here to work instead of taking on extra errands for cash would result in more time with the man I've become infatuated with, while also giving me some time to explore this Call.

"You're early, petal," Ellie says with a curious smile. "But it's perfect timing actually." Ellie-Mae steps out of her husband's embrace and moves over to me. "I'm actually just on my way out, but Beau here can show you what needs doin'. Does that suit you?"

I smile, feeling suspiciously set up but loving that these people care enough to play matchmaker for each other. "Does it suit Beau?" My eyes move to him, and he smirks.

"Any chance to be around you suits me, angel."

Biting the inside of my lip to stop myself from smiling any wider, I turn back to Ellie-Mae. "I'm sure we'll work really well together."

"OK. You've got my number if you need me," she says, touching my arm as she and Miller say their goodbyes and head off, leaving Beau and me alone.

"Where are they off to?" I ask, moving closer to where Beau is shifting pallets around.

"It's their date night. Randy is watchin' Whitney for them, and you and I are runnin' the store."

"So I'm like the second in charge or something?"

He grins at me and my insides turn to water. "Or somethin'."

"Need help with anything?" I ask, my voice amazingly steady considering my heart is beating out of my chest, my blood pulsing through my veins and sending my senses into hyper-drive.

Beau looks up at me, then nods toward the counter, a small smirk tugging his cheek up and dazzling me for a second.

"You're not needed back at the clinic?"

I shake my head. "Not today. Kendra works out at the horse rehab center on Tuesdays and Thursdays. So that's when I do some odd jobs around town. But I'm glad I have the chance to hang around here with you for a while. Until you guys don't need the help, anyway."

He rounds the counter and leans his hip into it, quirking his brow my way. "Hmm. You seem different today, angel. Why's that?"

My cheeks heat under his pointed stare, the desire to squirm on the spot growing the longer his eyes bore into mine. "No reason. I'm just having a good day. I like working here, truth be told." *And I love that I get to work with you some more too.*

He nods slowly. "Would you rather go home and relax before the kids get home from school? I can cover for you." A mischievous twinkle lights up his eyes and makes me grin *and* blush.

"Why would I wanna do that when I know I'd much rather spend time hangin' out with a cowboy at a supply store?" *Was that flirty? Ohmigod, that was* totally *flirty.* It's been so long since I've even had to care about flirting or dating and the like, I'd almost forgotten how fun it can be. *Oh well, I might as well run with it now.*

"Hmm." His eyes widen for just a second before a slow-growing sexy smile appears as tilts his head and scrubs his hand over his stubbled jaw as he pushes off the counter and starts walking toward me. "How about this? Instead of standing around behind the counter all afternoon, you help me restock the shelves with the new delivery that came in today, and not only do you get to spend time with *this* cowboy." *Thump. Thump. Thump.* "You're also gonna let me write off your debt for the car as a goodwill gesture." I open my mouth to protest, but just as he stops a foot away from me, he presses on, beating me to the punch at the same time he takes my damn breath away. "*Because* I'd much rather you come visit me at the ranch this weekend because you're ready to admit you wanna spend time with me."

*Wow. Is it getting hot in here? Beau Barnes continues to prove he's good at everything, even flirting.*

Without thinking about it, I lean forward, bringing us even closer. "You want to spend time with me?"

He chuckles, shaking his head as his eyes dance with amusement. "Angel, you're a smart woman. You know I wanna do more than just spend time with you. I wanna be the man by your side supporting you while you raise three awesome kids, working your three jobs, and still find time to be the beautiful, amazing, awe-inspiring woman standing in front of me right now."

I already knew I'd made a good choice coming here, but now I *know* I made the right decision.

"I think you're pretty amazing too, you know," I murmur, not wanting this moment to end. The world could implode around us outside this store, but I wouldn't even care because *this* with Beau, is filling my cup up more than I ever thought it would. *Why did you think you couldn't/shouldn't do this, Molly?*

"Where do you want me, boss?"

Beau's mouth drops open as he splutters and starts coughing. I swear I even catch the barest hint of a blush on his cheeks. *Yes, this is definitely going to be fun.*

"I *mean*, where do you want me to start first? Out the back? Or..." I look around the store, searching for any cartons that need unpacking.

Beau lifts his hand and rubs the back of his neck, a sexy smirk appearing along with one of his dimples that mesmerize me whenever I see them. "Maybe we should start with the hats."

"Sure thing, boss. Your wish is my command."

I go to walk past him toward the wall of hat hooks on the side of the store, but Beau's fingers curl gently around my bicep, his lips dropping close to my ear. "I'm gettin' the feelin' somethin's changed in you, Molly. And I'm likin' that change a hell of a lot, 'specially since I feel that wall of yours comin' down." I nod because my tongue feels like it's fused itself to the bottom of my mouth, my breath quickening and my skin so sensitized it feels burning hot. "But, just a warning, *friend* to *friend*, you keep calling me *boss*, and bein' a gentleman where you're concerned is gonna be damn near impossible." He growls low and slow in my ear, and I'm about to combust. *Holy moly.* This cowboy has my panties melting, and all he's doing is talking! This is just like my favorite flirty rom-com, but in real life, and Beau is the sexy alpha cowboy holding his true feelings back. In all the books I've read, usually that means that at some stage, he'll snap and just take what he wants. Just the thought has me fanning myself in my head.

I nod, my inner-romance lover swooning and squirming in her seat because yes, Beau's growling *totally* does things to me—things I definitely won't admit to right now—but also, I not only have butterflies, my tingles have tingles and my heart is doing its own little boot-scootin' boogie in my chest. And it's all because I'm opening myself up to the possibility that Kendra was right. Knowing that Beau is supposedly my soulmate—and vice versa—has made any reservations I had about pursuing this attraction between us fly out the window.

"Good. Now why don't you move your cute little tush over to the hats, and I'll go out to the storage cupboard and bring out the boxes for us to unpack?"

"OK," I say, grinning up at him, loving the way his gaze drops to my mouth and the rolling rumble in his chest that I hear when I lick my lips out of instinct.

"Be right back, angel."

"Sure thing, boss," I call out just as he disappears from view.

"Heard that."

"Maybe I wanted you too!" I yell back, giggling to myself and moving across the store as instructed, loving that after years of feeling alone and unable to let anyone in, suddenly, letting Beau in is *all* I want. I'm starting to believe I can be the woman who has it all.

A FEW HOURS LATER, we've worked our way through the delivery and restocked all the shelves, working side by side, sharing stories about growing up in Kinleyville and near the mountain. I'm not sure I've laughed and smiled this much in ages. I've also never felt as free and relaxed, not overthinking things, just being myself and going with the flow. And Beau—as he's done a lot in recent times—works hard to bring it out of me. He's just letting me be me, something I don't often get the opportunity to do. There's always something or someone needing my time and attention, so spending the afternoon with Beau actually turned into something kinda special.

Is *this* how the Call works? Just the thought that I could be the gift the Mountain Spirit wants to give Beau for his years of serving her and protecting the land is surreal enough. While walking over here, I couldn't help but look back over the past few weeks and all the time we've spent to-gether. And now knowing that there's more at play here than just a man and a woman liking each other, I'm kinda kicking myself that I've been so damn determined to keep him at a distance.

I look down at the last box of work boots at my feet, then back to the shelf in front of me, real-izing that there's no more room to squeeze even one more pair in there. "I don't think I can fit any-thing else. Is there a supply room where you store extra stock?" I ask.

"Sure. I can do that though if you need to be headin' off."

Shaking my head, I bend down and pick up the box, straightening and shooting him a coy smile. "I'm not in any rush. Colson is picking the other two up with my truck and goin' straight home."

He cocks a brow. "You weren't plannin' on walkin' home, were you? That's a hell of a hike, angel."

I bounce a shoulder. "It's quite nice. I've always liked the chance to stretch my legs and breathe in the mountain air."

"Well, how 'bout I do you one better and take you to Betty's for dinner to say thank you for doin' half my job."

My heart skips a beat, and I get a little thrill from the butterflies buzzing inside of me. "You know you don't have to thank me. I had fun. It was nice spendin' time with you today, Beau."

"Happy to hear that, 'cause you've made unpackin' stock a hell of a lot more enjoyable than it normally is."

I do a little curtsy. "Glad to be of service." Beau chuckles and moves toward me, nodding at the box in my hands.

"How 'bout I take that off your hands and leave it in the stockroom, and then we can head on out and have an early dinner? We can even grab extras to take home for the hoard." He shifts closer, a small smirk playing on his lips. "I promise to get your home by curfew, Miz Roberts."

His chocolate eyes look dark and melty this close up, and I kind of lose myself in them, my breathing becoming heavy as Beau's gaze slowly glides down to my lips then back up again, and suddenly it's like I've been lassoed by the cowboy and his entire being is pulling me in. Beau's eyes widen as I sway toward him and my lips part, my tongue darting out to wet them as I feel his warm breath fan over my skin. The jingle of the store's front door snaps me out of my daze and I jump back like I've been caught with my tongue down his throat. Not just *thinkin'* about doing it.

Beau mutters something unmentionable under his breath before turning toward the door. "I'll just be a minute, sir," he says to the male customer who just walked in before looking back at me.

"Lemme deal with him and we'll go, OK?"

I nod, my teeth digging into my lip and my hands fisting at my sides as I fight against every cell in my body which wants to fan myself while stamping my feet and cursing whatever being decided to interrupt our moment.

Because I thought Beau Barnes was about to kiss me, and I *wanted* him to. But maybe this is the Call's way. Maybe the Mountain Spirit likes to screw around with the couple first and play hard to get before letting us get to the good stuff... like kissing.

Kissing Beau stayed in the forefront of my mind while we waited for our food at Betty's, and when Beau rested his palm against the small of my back and led me down the main street of Kinleyville toward his truck. And it was still there the whole ride home as Beau made small talk, telling me how Sawyer's getting ready for the rodeo coming to town and talking about the upcoming breeding season at the ranch.

But even though I'm more than a little preoccupied, and have caught myself looking at Beau's mouth a *lot* more than could be deemed appropriate—or normal—by the time he pulls into my driveway, I can't help but feel a little disappointed. As much as I love coming home at the end of the day, it also means that my time alone with Beau is coming to an end.

Turning the engine off, he turns in his seat and I feel his gaze like a soft caress over the entire length of my body. I look over, my lips parting as I suck in a sharp breath, the hunger and desire reflecting back at me in his eyes the stuff dreams are made of. But then I realize that it's not the first time I've seen Beau look at me like that, it's just the first time I've let myself see it. And now that I've accepted that I want this man, I'm caught in what to do with that knowledge. *Do I tell him? Do I just keep acting normal and let him take the lead? Should I throw myself at him and hope he catches me?*

Leaning his arm against the steering wheel, he faces his body toward me, neither one of us able to look away. My chest tightens, my breathing labored the longer we sit there, the air in the car so thick I swear you could cut right through it.

Suddenly parched, I swipe the tip of my tongue along my bottom lip, earning a low, rumbling groan from Beau. Then it's as if it happens in slow motion, I shift forward an inch; he leans in a little; I move closer a little more, then Beau drapes his arm over the back of my seat, bringing his face almost within touching distance. *Omigod this is gonna happen.* I'm going to kiss Beau Barnes, and just the thought of that has my thighs clenching and my mouth watering.

And *God,* do I want it to happen. I wanna know what it feels like to have those perfect lips touch mine. I want to see if this is as scary and wonderful and as hot as hell as the promise of Beau Barnes seems to be.

A whimper escapes me when he cups my face in his hands and stares into my hooded gaze, his eyes asking an unspoken question that my jerky nod must answer, because the next thing I know, he's growling under his breath and lowering his lips to brush against mine. It's gentle at first, but I gasp at the electric spark that ignites throughout my body, my tongue darting out to touch his. My pulse spiking as his groan vibrates against my mouth the moment I open for him. And then finally... satisfyingly... Beau doesn't just kiss me... he *kisses* me. And for those glorious ten seconds of bliss, I teleport to another planet, another stratosphere where it's just me and him and we have no responsibilities, no one else to think about except the two of us, kissing and breathing, moaning, and whimpering, his fingers flexing against my jaw as mine digging into his shoulders, holding on for dear life.

It's just unfortunate that just when I let myself go and roll my tongue around his, the light on the front porch switches on, and we both freeze and turn our heads as we're met by Colson's knowing smirk as Sage and Cody flank him either side.

*Well, shit.*

"Think they've been waiting for you to get home?" I ask, laughing as I wave at the kids on the porch.

Molly shakes her head and rolls her eyes, the smile on her face not going anywhere, same as the flushed heat in her cheeks. "They're little devils. But I should get inside. Do my big sister duties." She moves to get out of the truck. "Thank you so much for today and tonight. It was nice spending some time just us."

"We'll have to do so more often."

Her teeth rake over her bottom lip as she nods. "I'd love that."

"Not comin' inside, Beau?" Colson calls out when Molly pushes the door open. "Ellie-Mae taught Sage her coffee recipe."

"That's mighty kind of you, but I should be headin' off. Early mornin'."

"Of course," he says. "Let me know if you need any help. I'll come out to the ranch whenever you need."

"Will do. Thanks, Cols."

He nods and all three of them give me a wave before he herds them back into the house and Molly is grinning ear to ear as she turns back to me. "I think my brother might be crushin' on you almost as hard as I am."

"This is just a crush, is it?" I tease, grinning right back. "Here I was thinkin' this was the Mountain's doin'."

"The Call," she says on a breath, and I nod.

"Definitely more than a crush on my side, angel. It's important to me that you know that."

"You're right. This feels...big. Life changin'."

"You think you're ready for somethin' like that?"

Inhaling a deep breath, she releases it before meeting my gaze again, this time with a glint in her eye that wasn't there before. "I think I am...*boss*."

I don't know what it is about her calling me that, but a deep rumble reverberates out of my chest in response. "I warned you 'bout usin' that name for me."

"You did. It's precisely why I'm gonna keep saying it." She giggles and steps away from the truck while I growl again. "Good night, Beau."

"Good night, Molly. I'll see you real soon."

"I hope so," she says, before closing the door and heading toward the house, putting a little extra sway in her step that my dick most definitely appreciates, but my heart appreciates even more. Because she's lowering her walls. She's letting me in. And I couldn't be happier about that.

"WHOA-HO! WHAT IS THIS SMILE ABOUT?" Kendra leans into Jesse as she tilts her beer up to me in greeting when I approach the firepit. All the brothers are gathered, along with Kendra and El-lie-Mae, who has a baby monitor sitting right next to her so she can watch Whitney sleeping inside the ranch house.

"Let's just say Ellie-Mae's meddling was appreciated," I say, completely unable to wipe the smile that's made its home on my face ever since Molly and I kissed.

Ellie-Mae kicks up her feet and claps while she squeals excitedly. "I'm so happy right now! I *knew* that all you needed was a little time alone to move things along."

"Question is, how far did you move things along?" Sawyer asks, waggling his brow and making me laugh. I take a seat next to him and grab a beer.

"We kissed," I admit, and both Kendra and Ellie-Mae gasp while my brothers all smirk. Sawyer just tilts his head slightly. "What? That's not enough for you?"

"Don't ask 'im that," Randy puts in. "He'll start braggin' about how amazin' he is at talkin' girls out of their panties."

"Hey, I have a talent, and I'm not afraid to use it," Sawyer says, brushing imaginary dirt off his shoulders before I give him a friendly punch in the arm. "You guys should've asked me for pointers long ago."

"Just you wait, brother. When you meet your One and you get to that first kiss." I sigh like a love-struck teenager. "It's amazin'. Better than any other kiss, ever."

Sawyer's brows lift as he takes a drink. "Like, how? Kissin's kissin'. It's the precursor to the good stuff. Why're you swoonin' like a teenage girl with a crush over a kiss?"

I sit back, trying to think about how to describe it in a way that might get through to Mr. wham-bam-see-you-later man over there. "A regular kiss feels good and all. But kissin' Molly, it's like my soul joined in. I don't know how else to describe it. Something shifted in me and I never wanted it to end."

He chuckles in disbelief. "Your *soul* joined in?"

"He's right," Miller says. "That's exactly how it feels." He looks to the side, and the three heads of Jesse, Kendra, and Ellie-Mae bob in agreement.

"Hmm." Sawyer tosses his bottle back and drains it while Kendra sits forward and taps my knee.

"So, Molly is starting to come around, huh? What's the next step?" she asks.

"A date, I guess. Or something special for her that doesn't involve work for a change."

"Her birthday is coming up this weekend. Maybe you could do something special for that?"

"Oh yes!" Ellie-Mae jumps in, her eyes lighting up. "We can even help you plan if you like. You can romance the boots off the girl and sweep her off her feet in the process."

I chuckle as I remove the cap from my bottle. "I just might take you up on that," I say, taking a drink before catching the thoughtful expression on Sawyer's face. "Hey, Kendra? You got any seer knowledge about when Sawyer's Call is coming?"

"Oh no," she says with a laugh. "We're not doing that. Even if I did know—which I don't yet—I couldn't tell you. He's gonna have to recognize it and accept it himself, same as you."

Randy chuckles from beside me. "It's gonna be a shit show," he says, causing Sawyer to scowl.

"You think I can't work it out?" Sawyer shoots his way.

"I think it's gonna scare the shit outta you and you're gonna hightail it in the opposite direction."

Sawyer picks up a new bottle and shakes his head. "I don't know why we're all so focused on me here when it isn't even my turn, and probably won't be for months and months. Maybe even years. So how 'bout we drop it and keep the conversation on Beau and Molly where it belongs?"

"Maybe because Beau and Molly are doing great together all on their own," Kendra says. "For my first couple to guide as the Eagle Mountain seer, I couldn't be more relieved it's all starting to work out."

"You think we can start plannin' their weddin'?" Ellie-Mae asks, giving me a wink to let me know she's teasing.

"Maybe," Kendra says with a slow nod. "If things keep going as well as they are, we just might have wedding bells by the end of Summer."

"That's a bit sudden, don't you think?" I say, laughing at how carried away they're all getting.

"Oh, I don't think so," Kendra says, looking at Jesse, who gives her a warm and loving smile. "Once you've completed the Call, there doesn't seem a lot of sense in waiting." She turns back to me. "But every couple is different. And you have to go at your own pace. Just know, we're all rooting for you to have an uncomplicated Call from here on out."

"From your lips to the Mountain Spirit's ears," I say, necking the rest of my drink.

## 17

# MOLLY

"You look like sunshine on a platter, Miss Molly," Mr. Gibson says as he comes up to the reception desk after his cat's check-up.

"They do tell me I brighten up a room. I think it's the blonde hair." His responding infectious laugh makes my smile shine brighter.

"True, true. Glad to see you smiling though," he says.

I smile and play it coy, not about to tell one of my favorite clients the reason behind my good mood. It's safe to say I've been walking on air since my brief, but no less mind-blowing kiss with Beau in my driveway, all ten seconds of it. It was the single best moment of my life. The best kiss, the best *everything*. That can only mean *other* things will be just as good, right? Of course, Colson and Sage were shooting me knowing looks over breakfast this morning since the kids caught us in the act, but the thought that I might get another chance to kiss Beau again soon far outweighs any embarrassment I feel over having the moment seen by my entire family.

I keep catching myself watching the clock, willing time to go faster so I can get home and get ready. I'm not sure I've ever been *this* enthusiastic about having to work a shift at the Lair since I started there. Mr. Gibson's cat, Dusty, is the last patient of the day, so all that's left to do is finish up and get out the door. Because tonight, even though I'm working, I'll also get to see Beau. Wednesday night is for boot-scootin' 'round here, after all.

"Well, then. Whatever it is, I hope it continues, missy. I'm glad you're smiling again," Mr. Gibson continues, fixing up his bill and shooting me a wave before bending down to grab his cat cage and walking out of the clinic.

"He's right, you know," Kendra says, appearing out of nowhere beside me.

A startled squeak escapes me. "Whoa, sneak up on a girl, why don't ya?"

"Maybe you were too busy clock watching and thinking about a certain cowboy to notice me?" she says with an arched brow.

"Maybe." I shake my head. "I'm no different than normal. I'm just having a good day. Maybe I'm enjoying my job."

The look Kendra shoots me is nothing short of skeptical. "*Right*. And I'm a monkey's uncle."

I place my hand on my chest and gasp. "You are?"

My best friend narrows her eyes, her lips twitching as she rounds the desk and takes the spare seat beside me. "So what's new?"

"Nothin..."

"Again... what's *new*, Molly Roberts?"

A resigned sigh escapes me as I shut down my computer and turn to face her, a little suspicious now. She is a Seer, after all, and I've read enough of Aster's books to know that Seers can communicate with the Mountain Spirit. Which means she knows things. Which *could* mean that she knows things that she isn't telling me. "Can I ask you something?"

"Anything, babe. You know that. If I *can* tell you something, I will."

"See, that's what's a little confusing to me. If you *know* that Beau and I are destined to be together, then why didn't you tell me way back when you first found out? Or at least when you told me to pull my head out of my butt and stop holding back?"

Her gaze gentles. "Unfortunately, it doesn't work like that. I can see things in my dreams, but I don't see *everything*. So I'm not gonna lie and tell you that I haven't known for a while, but the Call isn't as simple as putting the man and his soul-mate together and *boom*, all is well. It's a journey, Molls, and there's always a purpose to why the Mountain Spirit does the things she does. I'm just a guide who's here to help you past the bumps in the road."

"Like what?"

"Well, you know how I went to Canada to work at the horse rehab center?" I nod. I never under-stood why she chose to move away from the man she loved, just as it seemed like they were finding their way together. Thankfully, as promised, Kendra came back and now she and Jesse are married and more in love than ever. To be honest, seeing her fall head over heels for her cowboy, and watching the way he looks at her like she's the only sun shining in his sky, has been kind of inspiring to me. It's given my romantic heart hope that one day, I too might find a love that strong and true.

And until recently, even though I knew there was this insane and inexplicable attraction between

Beau and me, I didn't think it was my time. But now... and after that kiss... I can't help but hope that the Mountain Spirit has got it right and that Beau and I *are* meant to be.

Ironic that just last week, I was still holding the man at arm's length and now I'm sitting here desperate to see him again. It's like I've been starving myself, and now I want it all.

Kendra continues, bringing me back to the present. "I went away because I *needed* to. Not to get away from Jesse, but to follow my dreams, and to see that I could have my dream *and* the man I love. And as hard as it was—and believe me, it was so damn difficult to be so far away from you all—looking back, I wouldn't change my journey for anything because look at me now; married, making my dream of a horse rescue a reality, *and* I have family and friends supporting me through it all."

"Yeah, you do." I reach out and hug her. "And I'm so damn proud of you too."

"I want that for you too, Molls. But I can't tell you how that is gonna happen for you because the Spirit hasn't shown me that. Not yet, anyway."

"So until then, I'm on my own?"

"Oh no. I can tell you about the Mountain Lore, well, what you don't already know."

I lean back in my chair, giving her my full attention. "OK, then. Hit me with the goods, oh wise one."

"Smartass," she quips.

"Yes, ma'am."

"Well, it started with the Coopers over on Moose Mountain, and then the birth of a baby to the only Cooper daughter activated the spirit for the nine founding brothers at the Bear Mountain Homestead, one of which Miller, Ellie-Mae's husband."

"And let me guess, when they had Whitney, it activated the spirit at Eagle Mountain for Jesse and his brothers?"

She nods. "Now you're getting it."

"OK. So I understand all of that. But how does the Mountain Spirit choose *which* brother hears the Call and when? And *who* their chosen partner, soulmate, *whatever* is?"

"Their One. That's what they are."

"Like their one and only?" I say with a wry grin.

"Yep. And there's no way of knowing who will hear the Call. Sometimes it works through from oldest to youngest, but mostly, from what I've been told, there's no rhyme or reason as to *who* on the mountain hears the Call and when."

"And what about the One? How did Jesse know it was you? How did you know it was Jesse?"

"And how are you to know that it's *you* who is meant to be for Beau?" she says, sensing my unasked question.

"Yeah..." I whisper.

"That's what my visions are for. But at the end of the day, you just know. It's in the way you feel when you think of him, the way your body reacts when you're near each other, the way you look at each other. You just..."

"You just know, right?"

"You sure do, because as soon as you realize it, that's when the feelings you've had, the nev-erending thoughts about one another, the strong pull to be together, ramps up until you can't be-lieve you fought it."

"Did you fight it?"

She laughs and shakes her head. "For all of about a second, babe. The Call is more than a little per-suasive."

"What do I do then?"

"You follow your heart, you listen to your soul, and you keep an open mind, and you'll see what happens. But if you listen to anything I say, I want you to take this to heart—whatever happens, that man will never hurt you. He'll support you, cheer you on, and be at your back whether you think you need someone in your corner or not. He's totally hooked on you, Molly. Now it's time to let him know that you're just as hooked as he is."

I let her words roll around my head for a moment before I lean in, my voice dropping to a whisper. "I really like him, Kendie. Maybe too much."

Her smile is almost as blinding as mine. "I'm not sure there's such a thing as too much where the Call's concerned. But that's why we're all coming to the Lair tonight for a drink. It means you and Beau get time together—even if you're working—and Jesse and I can stand back and watch someone *else* go through the Call." She stands up and stops in the doorway to look back at me. "And since we're all finished here, I think it's time for you to head on home and get ready. You have a smitten cowboy that's been grinning almost as much as you all week who's looking forward to seeing you. And since I know you so well, something tells me you're gonna go all out tonight to make sure you have his complete attention."

My mouth drops open because she's absolutely right. *Damn Seer abilities.*

"You know it's annoyin' knowin' you know what's gonna happen, and I don't, right?"

"Yes, ma'am. But don't worry, Beau is just as frustrated as you are." And with a parting wink, she walks down the hall.

"*So* annoyin'!" I call out with a laugh.

"Yep. But it'll be worth it, babe. Trust me in that."

That's when I finish what I have to do and rush out the door, because I may have to work, but now I *really* can't wait to see Beau again.

And hopefully kiss him again. Because every girl knows, ten seconds is *never* enough.

## 18

## BEAU

If watching Molly from across the room were an Olympic sport, I'd surely have a gold medal by now. I've spent all night with my eyes glued to her movements, sharing secret knowing glances whenever we lock eyes.

"Get ya ass on the dancefloor, brother," Sawyer says, his chest heaving after yet another round of kicking up his boots. He picks up his beer and drinks thirstily. "Your girl is goin' on a break soon, so you might get the chance to pull her in for a whip around the dancefloor too."

"How do you know that?" I ask, narrowing my eyes.

He grins. "Asked Eric for ya. You're welcome."

Shaking my head, I grin right back. "Thank you, Sawyer."

"No problem. Just don't tell anyone. Can't have them thinkin' I've gone soft all of a sudden. Got a reputation to protect and all that." He gives me a wink and I chuckle.

"Secret's safe with me, bro. No one will ever know you're a romantic at heart."

He barks out a laugh before he downs the last of his drink then drags me out onto the dancefloor where *Country Girl* by Luke Bryan has started playing. Sawyer and I slide in next to Randy and Jesse, tapping our boots and clapping our hands in time with the rhythm, and just as he starts singing about the girls shaking it, I spot Molly without her apron standing on the sideline and just have to pull her in.

She lands against my chest, her face upturned in laughter as I keep us moving with the line so we're not in anyone else's way. "You gonna shake it for me, country girl?" I tease, earning a bright smile as Molly makes space for herself in front of me, spinning and *shaking* everything she's got for my viewing pleasure. She seems so free and happy, that all I can think about is making her feel like this all the time. I want to be the man to protect and care for her, the man who provides for and supports her. I want to be the light in her life and take the burden off her shoulders. I want to love her with everything I have. I want to be everything she needs and wants in a man.

When the song finishes, I catch Molly by the hand and slow dance with her for a moment before I walk her off the dancefloor. "Where are we goin?" she yells over the loud music.

"We're gonna take some food up to the roof so you can have some quiet and get off your feet durin' your break," I say, swinging past the bar and picking up the food I asked Eric to have ready so I could make sure my woman gets fed.

"You're too good to me, Beau," she says as I lead her up the stairs to the private area only a handful of patrons get the use of.

"All that does is tell me nobody's ever treated you right before, angel." I kiss her temple as we step out onto the rooftop, taking a seat at a picnic table set out under a bunch of fairy lights behind the Lair's fluorescent sign. The night is cool but feels mighty fine on your skin after having the heat of dancing bodies pressing in on you. Molly takes a deep breath and sighs happily.

"I like it up here," she says.

"Great view of the mountain."

"And it's romantic." She pops a piece of fried chicken in her mouth and chews.

"Yeah. I'll give it that," I say, looking around at the potted plants that have been set up here to add to the ambiance.

"Almost like a mini-date."

"Gotta squeeze them in where we can, right?"

She sighs and meets my eyes. "Yeah. And I love that you work with me, Beau. I can't tell you how much I appreciate the patience you've shown."

I nod my understanding as I clasp my hands in front of me and just watch the woman eat. She seems voracious, and it only solidifies my earlier need to be the man who takes care of her and makes sure she looks after herself in the process. She has a habit of just leaning forward and making her feet scramble to catch up. I can only imagine how exhausting that must be for her day in and day out, so I take great pleasure in successfully getting her to sit for a moment, eat in peace, and just breathe.

"You want some?" she asks, her cheeks full as she pushes her plate toward me.

I shake my head. "I ate earlier. That's all yours, angel."

She grins. "I'm kinda glad about that. I'm starved. I might've forgotten to eat today."

"You tellin' me I have to start bringin' you lunch too?"

Her eyes lift to mine and hold. "You'd do that too, wouldn't you?"

"In a heartbeat."

Wiping her hands on her napkin, she lifts her lemonade to her lips and takes a sip. "Swoon," she says once she swallows, laughter in her eyes.

"Got you swoonin' huh?" I lean forward with my arms folded in front of me as she nods.

"From the moment you gave me the time of day, if I'm honest. Problem was, and still is, my available time." She reaches across the table and places her hand on mine. "I want this to work, Beau. I really do. But is this"—she gestures between us, at the food on the table and the rooftop of the Lair— "what you want? Is it gonna be enough, because I'm not sure I have much more to give right now."

"What I want," I say, lifting her hand to mine and pressing a kiss to her knuckles, "is you. And I'll take that however you wanna give it to me. In whatever form I can get it."

She hums lightly as she smiles, moving her hand back to her side of the table to continue eating. "So, what time are you and your brothers leaving?"

"They'll head off when the sun sets, I guess. I drove here separately so I can hang around till the end of your shift. Maybe walk you to your car."

"Yeah?"

I nod.

"You are just too good to me, Beau Barnes," she says again, shaking her head like she's trying to come to terms with what's happening here.

"You keep comin' back to that, but I'm not gonna stop treatin' you like a queen, angel. As far as I'm concerned, when a man sets his sights on a woman—whether it's the Call bringin' them together or not—he needs to set a standard and treat her so great, she'll wonder how she ever got by without you in her life."

"I'm already startin' to think that, boss."

"Then keep thinkin' it," I say, just as an alarm goes off on her wristwatch and she lets out a sigh as she stops it.

"I've gotta get back down there," she says, rising with her plate in hand. "Thank you so much for this little reprieve. It's the best work break I've ever had."

"See you soon," I say, watching her as she heads back down the stairs while I take a moment longer to sit in the quiet of the roof. You can still hear the music from inside the Lair, but it's so muted that it feels like it's much farther away than just a floor below. Seems the *Watermelon Crawl* is playing, and I grin to myself, knowing how much both Jesse and Sawyer love that one. I think it's because it's got some of the easiest foot-work out of all the dances we do here. Even Miller, the worst dancer out of all of us, has managed to get the hang of this one.

And then my mind turns right back to Molly, my hopes and dreams for a future with her, and the fact that she still has the shadow of a wall up between us that's telling me she still isn't one hundred percent sure she can let herself have something with me while she's still providing and caring for her siblings. *Seems I still have some convincing to do.*

But I'm nothing if not persistent, so I guess the mountain made the right call bringing us together.

After heading back down to the bar, I join in with a few more dances with my brothers, then they all head off and I hang back to wait for Molly, chatting to some locals outside while she finishes up.

"Thought you might have gotten tired and gone home," she says when she finds me out there, bag over her shoulder and coat in hand.

"Never. I said I'd be here, so I am. You can count on me, angel."

"I'm starting to see that," she says, looping her arm inside mine as I walk her across the parking lot to her truck in slow and comfortable silence.

"I think I should probably apologize for my nosey siblings interrupting us last night," Molly says once we reach the truck and I take the keys from her to unlock it.

"Why's that?"

"They interrupted a..." She presses her lips together and even in the dim light of the setting sun, I can see the blush creeping over her cheeks. "a *moment*."

"Oh, angel. We're gonna have plenty of those moments," I say, lifting a hand to cup the side of her face before lowering my mouth to hers, brushing our lips until she opens for me, and I kiss her the way I've been dying to since my heart started beating only for her.

My hand moves to the back of her head, cradling her as my tongue sweeps through her mouth, tasting cool lemonade as she whimpers and wraps her arms around my neck. She lets me take control, alternating the pressure between a devouring need and a gentle taste as my hands start to roam down to her ass, pulling her against me so she can feel just how hot and hard she makes me, how much I physically crave her, *need* her, even though my spirit seems to be in the driver's seat.

"Oh my god, Beau," she moans, her fingers clawing at my shirt. "How are we gonna do this? How are we gonna find the time to make anythin' but a stolen kiss happen?"

Pulling back slightly, I move my hands to either side of her face and look deep into her eyes. "We'll find a way, Molly. I'm prepared to love you however you need to be loved, and before you go thinkin' you owe me anythin' in return, you need to know I expect nothin'. All I want is for you to let me in. Let me show you I'm your man."

"Beau," she whispers, closing her eyes against a glistening emotion. "You have no idea how many nights I've prayed for a man like you."

I lower my forehead to hers and take a deep breath. "Then the Mountain heard you, angel. She heard me too. Because you're exactly what I've always wanted too." She releases a slight whimper as I bring my mouth to hers again, kissing her slow and soft this time before I pull back, then open up her truck door. "I should let you go and get some rest."

"OK, boss," she whispers, teasing me as she gets into the truck and looks up at me. "I'll see you at the supply store tomorrow?"

I touch her lightly on the chin. "Sure will."

"And on Saturday at the ranch."

"You sure you wanna work the ranch on your birthday?"

Her eyes widen. "How'd you know?"

"Kendra," I say, and she nods in complete understanding.

"Of course, she let it slip. I normally just let it slide on by without much fanfare. So yeah, I'm more than happy to spend the day with you and the kids ranching. It's kind of our thing, right?"

"Yeah, angel, it's totally our thing," I say, as I close her into the truck and step back, waving her off after yet another all-consuming-but-never-enough-moment that proves to me I will literally do *anything* to make that woman mine.

## 19

## MOLLY

Turning twenty-four isn't much different from the day I turned twenty-three... or yesterday, for that matter. The kids woke me up with breakfast and coffee in bed.

Cody gave me a wooden jewelry box he'd made with Colson's help to use Dad's tools in the garage. They looked up how to do it on the internet at the Kinleyville Library and then stole time away whenever I was working late so it could be a surprise.

Sage gave me a painting she'd done on canvas at school of a beautiful sunset with Eagle Mountain as a backdrop. It was stunning and brought a tear to my eye, which of course earned me a typical teenage eye roll, but I could also tell she was proud of what she'd created.

Colson gave me a book of coupons he'd made, many of which were of the "let Colson do something for me so I can relax" persuasion. Seems he's been taking lessons from Beau on that front.

And since it's my birthday, it also meant Eric gave me a paid night off, so the kids have told me they've organized the cake and dinner tonight so there's nothing for me to do. I feel spoiled.

But what I'm really looking forward to most is heading out to the ranch and spending the day with Beau and the kids. Even though Beau said my debt was written off, it's kind of become a tradition now for all of us Roberts' to pile into my truck and drive out there every Saturday morning. The kids love it; *I* love it, and the bonus of it all is that I get to see Beau—oh, and Kendra and the rest of them too. *But mostly Beau.*

As soon as we arrive, Kendra rushes my door, swinging it wide open with a huge smile on her face and pulling me in for a big hug. "Happy Birthday!" she announces to all and sundry, making my cheeks heat up as I hop down from the truck.

"Happy Birthday, Molls," Jesse says, coming up beside Kendra and wrapping an arm around her waist.

"I like to think it's just like any other day, but thanks, guys."

Then it's like a whole damn welcoming committee appears, Sawyer, Randy, Ellie-Mae, Miller, and even little Whitney, all coming outside to join us in a chorus of 'happy birthday.' Then I see Beau, and it's like every single cell in my body buzzes with excitement. He walks over and we stand there, staring at each other, not uttering a word, the thick air between us saying it all.

"C'mon, kids. I've got some biscuits and sausage gravy leftover from breakfast if you'd like some," Ellie-Mae says, ushering everyone back inside and leaving me and Beau alone.

Then he's pulling me in for a hug that's so warm and tight and what might just be up there on the list of best birthday presents ever, his lips moving to my ear. "Happy Birthday, angel," he murmurs, making me shudder out a shaky breath when he presses a soft, reverent kiss against my neck.

"It is now."

Shifting back, he holds me close in his arms and smiles down at me.

"What're our plans for today then, boss," I ask, earning a knowing smirk and a low husky laugh.

"Was thinking we'd shuck out the stalls in the barn, maybe help Kendra and Jesse out with repairing a few fences at the Horse Haven, then we'll come back here for your birthday dinner."

"My birthday dinner?"

"Kids didn't tell you?"

I laugh and shake my head. "They said it was organized, but not by who. Wow. You've all been so welcoming and inclusive. Sometimes I feel like I'll never be able to repay any of y'all for your kindness."

He leans in and brushes his lips against mine in a barely there kiss. "I'll let you in on a little secret, angel."

"What's that?" I ask back breathlessly.

"Seeing you happy and smiling is all the thanks we'll ever need."

I cock my head and arch a brow. "You don't want any special, private thanks?"

"Well, now. There're *plenty* of private things I'd like to do with you. But that's all about mutual give and take, never about owing."

I laugh and smile up at him. "OK, OK. I get it, boss. I don't *owe* you anything. But what if I *want* to do things for you—to you?"

He tightens his grip on me and brushes his nose alongside mine. "Well, angel, I'd say that's a discussion I'll gladly have with you later." He kisses me again, but this time it's not just a lip touch, there's tongue and teeth and it's utterly *divine*. But unfortunately, we're interrupted yet again... Not by my brother this time, instead it's by something bumping into my leg.

"What in the world?" I ask, laughing when we both look down to find Gertie the goat staring up at me, a leather glove hanging from her mouth, before he spins on his hooves and runs away with a happy bleat.

I glance back to Beau. "I guess we will have to continue this conversation later."

His eyes darken and *oh yes*, there's definitely a high chance of this birthday girl getting kisses and *more* in the near future. "You can count on it, angel. Now let's go save my glove from that damn goat before she eats it and dinner turns into goat curry instead of Ellie's Beef Pot Roast."

THAT NIGHT after a delicious home-cooked meal fit for a Queen, and a birthday cake covered in lemon frosting and sprinkles, we all move outside and sit around the fire pit with a beer in our hands as we watch the twilight sky morph into night right in front of us. Conversation flows like water into the ocean, and the guys give each other shit as these brothers always seem to do. The kids are mucking around with the goat and Kendra's amazing cat, Spencer. Cody is determined to teach Spencer a new trick he feels is even better than riding on horseback—riding on *goat-back*.

"Wanna take a walk?" Beau murmurs in my ear as I lean up against him.

I turn to meet his warm brown eyes that remind me of a pool of chocolate I just wanna dive into and never come up for air. *How apt that it's exactly what I wanna do with Beau.* I nod and slide my hand into his as he stands and mutters a gruff "be back soon" before leading me around the side of the ranch house.

"Where are we going?" I ask curiously.

"Just gimme a minute, angel," he says, his voice low and deep and all kinds of rumbly. *Yum.*

When we reach the back of the barn, he stops and turns to face me, barely giving me time to register the look of complete and unadulterated heat in his gaze before his hands are cradling my face, his body is pressed against mine, and he's walking me backward until my shoulders touch the wall.

He dips his forehead to rest against mine, his breath fanning over my lips in a teasing caress that makes me want to jump the man and ride him all the way home. *Whoa, down girl!*

"Hey," he murmurs.

"Hey."

"I've been countin' down the hours till I could get you all to myself again," he says with a smile, lifting his head and letting his half-lidded gaze wander over my features.

My lips quirk up. "Well, it looks like you got what you wish for. So *now* that you have me, what're you gonna do with me?"

"What I've been wanting to do ever since I saw you this mornin'," he growls. Then his lips crash down onto mine, and all I can do is wrap my arms around his shoulders and hold on as he plunders my mouth like a pillaging pirate, kissing me with a desperation that matches my own.

I slide my fingers up into his hair, holding him to me as I lift a leg and wrap it around his thigh, lifting on my toes trying to get impossibly close.

"Fuck, angel. You drive me crazy. I want you so bad I can barely breathe."

"Then have me," I whimper before grabbing his head and kissing him again, wanting to fuse my lips to his so that we never have to stop. My blood is boiling, my body burning up with every stroke of his tongue. It's too much and not enough all at the same time.

"I wanna taste you. I want to feel you under my tongue as I drive you crazy and make you come so hard you see stars," he murmurs, dragging his lips down my neck and nipping at my throat.

"Please," I beg, rolling my hips against the tantalizing bulge in his jeans. "Please, Beau. I need…"

"I'm gonna take care of you, angel," he says between kisses. "I'm gonna make you feel real good, yeah?"

"*Yes.*" I can barely breathe with how much I want this man right here, right now. It's reckless, it's wild, but it also seems so damn overdue. "Please, Beau."

"I've got you, Molly," he says, running his hands down my shirt and rolling my hard nipples between his fingers, my back arching at the exquisite pleasure that jolts straight down to my core.

My breath catches and my heart pounds as my big, gruff cowboy leans in and gives me a deep, hard kiss with lots of tongue before shooting me a sexy grin and dropping to his knees, his hands moving to my jeans as his deft fingers make quick work of opening my fly and pulling the denim down to my ankles. Then with his dark, lust-filled eyes locked with mine, he buries his face between my legs, his tongue swiping the full length of me before he wraps his lips around my clit. I moan so loud, I scare myself and quickly slap my hand over my mouth, struggling to keep my eyes open and on the man with a tongue so talented it should be outlawed.

He licks, sucks, and kisses me, relentless in his pursuit for pleasure, the rest of the world around us the last thing on my mind. All I care about is the way he moves his tongue just... right... there, over and over again, swirling, circling, dipping lower and spearing the tip inside me, his guttural groan vibrating against my sensitive skin, sending me higher and higher.

"Yes," I whimper as one of Beau's hands shifts to grip my hip, the other moving between my legs as he slowly pushes two fingers inside of me at the same time he sucks my clit between his lips. Then I'm done for, my vision going white, my head slamming back against the barn as I dig my teeth into my palm and scream out my climax, a tsunami of pleasure washing over me, my body shaking with the pleasure that just keeps going on and on. Beau slowly eases me back down to earth, placing a soft kiss at the top of my mound before carefully righting my jeans and doing them up again.

As soon as he's standing in front of me again, I grab his face and pull him to me, slamming my mouth on his and thanking him *thoroughly* by pouring everything I have into that kiss, my soul so light and free that I'm near floating on air.

"Fucking beautiful when you let go, angel."

A hot blush warms my cheeks and I bury my face in his neck, smiling against his skin while his hands move up and down my back in soft, slow strokes. "Now, for your present."

"That wasn't it?" I ask with a smirk.

"No." He chuckles. "I wanna take you somewhere. On a date, a real one. Just you and me. Whaddaya say?"

For a second I let the warm gooey feeling wash over me while I think of what it would be like to live out my fantasy of going on a date with Beau Barnes. But then the ice bucket of reality slaps me in the face as what just happened and what we just did sinks in.

*Ohmigod. What did I just... out here... when the kids are... shit.* What if they'd come looking and found me like that?

"What happened to being happy snatching date-like moments on rooftops, Beau? I can't just abandon the kids because I've decided to take up with you," I say, a little sharper than intended, my sudden panic dictating my actions. The moment the words are out of my mouth and his muscles tense under my touch, I realize I've screwed up. "Shit. I'm sorry."

He straightens and looks down at me, his gaze turning wary with an edge of frustration you can't miss in it. "Your siblings are seventeen, fifteen, and eleven, Molly. They can handle you going on a date. Hell, you've got a whole ranch full of people willin' to sit with them if you don't think they should be alone."

"It's not that, Beau. It's—"

"It's what? I just told you I wanna spend time with you, angel. I want to *be* with you. And I thought you'd enjoy getting away from it all for a night, letting me treat you the way I promised I would. I thought we were past this." He pulls his lips between his teeth as he rakes his fingers through his hair and shakes his head, shifting away from me. "You still can't see it can you?"

My spine stiffens, my body going ramrod straight. "Can't see what?"

"This—us—this isn't me flirting with you, spending time with your family and mine, buttering you up because I want you in my bed. This is more than that. I want the chance to be everything you'll ever want and need, Molly."

"I know that, Beau. And I want that too. But I can't pretend that I'm a twenty-four-year-old woman who doesn't have responsibilities. I can't just sneak away for a night, or sneak behind a barn to do this, knowing the kids aren't far away and could come by looking for us." I don't know who I'm trying to convince now, because my resistance is waning faster than it took for Beau to make me cry out his name.

"Never asked you to pretend. Never asked anything of you except for you to give me a chance. A real one, without you coming up with reasons why we can't be together."

"But I have to pretend, Beau. I have to because this can't be real. It's too much. You're too wonderful, and I'm...." I shake my head to try and fight the tears. "Fairytales aren't real. Life has more than shown me that, or I wouldn't have three kids to take care of on my own. And I promised, Beau. I promised my dad I'd look after them, that I'd keep the family together. And if I go chasing my own heart, it'll change things for them and I'm trying, I'm trying to do what's right for them *and* me, but it's hard, Beau. It's so hard."

"Then let me help you, Molly. Let me *in*. I'm just tryin' to love you. I don't want to pretend anything when you are the only thing I can think about." He presses his hard body against mine, my breath catching as my body heats up again, my pulse spiking at the feel of all of him up against me again. Dipping his chin, he leans in until he's all I can see, his dark eyes staring deep into mine as he brings his mouth to mine and kisses me hard and deep. "This is *real*."

"I—" I shake my head and worry my bottom lip in my teeth. "I know this is real, Beau. I know this is big. Maybe even *too* big for me to handle. The way I feel about you, it's... *huge*."

He takes my hand and places it over his heart so I can feel it thumping against his chest, right in time with mine. "And I'm right there with you. I've never felt this way about anyone in my entire life, and now it's like I can never get enough of you. And it's scary, and strange, and hard to wrap your head around, because we're expected to believe some Mountain Spirit has swooped in and decided to bring us together. So, I get it. But if it means I get *you*, knowing that this feels so damn right, then to me it's the most natural thing in the world."

"But...but what if I'm not ready yet? What if the Mountain was wrong? What if I let you in and everything comes crashing down? What happens then? Because I can tell you now, I'm not strong enough to lose everything I love again."

"I won't let you down, Molly. Can't you see that? I'm here. I'm right here, and I'm not going anywhere."

Tears sting my eyes as the loss of my mother, the loss of my father, the loss of *everything* I knew to be love, swirls around inside me like a brewing storm. The idea of loving Beau, of counting on him, leaning on him, seems so right but also so frightening that I'm scared to be more than we are right now. Because right now, everything is safe. The kids are safe. My heart is safe. And nothing too huge has changed. But if I fall into this, into *him,* then everything does change. And what happens to my siblings when they fall in love with him and rely on him too? What happens if something happens to him? What happens if this doesn't work out?

What happens to us on the other side of this big love he's promising me?

"I...I'm not ready, Beau," I whisper as a tear makes its way down my cheek.

His eyes roam my face, his expression gentle but saddened. "Then I'm sorry for pushin' you," he says, letting out his breath as he takes a step back, then another, my heart aching the further away he gets from me, the distance feels like a gaping chasm.

"Beau," I say, my heart feeling like a weight in my chest as I regret every single word that just came out of my stupid, frightened mouth. *Why am I chasing away the best thing that's ever happened to me?*

"I'll walk you back," he mutters gruffly, and I'm suddenly hit with a wave of panic that this might be the moment that Beau decides I might not be worth the trouble.

No, no, no, no. I can't lose this man. Whatever this is, it's important, it's precious, it's something bigger than all of us. The Mountain Spirit wouldn't choose wrong. I've read all the books, it's *never* wrong. I am. And I'm letting my fear of abandonment get in the way of something amazing.

Without thinking any further, I surge forward, closing my eyes and putting every ounce of trust I have in this man and the mystic being that brought us together.

"I lied," I blurt, grabbing his hand before he can get too far. "I want this. I want you, and I believe the Mountain called us to each other. So that's a guaranteed happy ever after, right? I'm just...I'm scared out of my ever-loving mind here. Please don't let me push you away. Please don't give up on me, Beau. Please." I'm desperate, hoping and praying that he can see just how much I mean it.

"Fuck, angel. *Fuck.* I got you. I've always got you." Then I'm wrapped up in my strong cowboy's arms, sealing our fate with a kiss that puts all of those before it to shame. "I will never, ever give up on you. You hear me?"

I nod. Knowing that whatever happens next, there's no way I want this night to end. I've skirted the edge of losing him, and I just can't, I can't walk away and I can't keep holding back. Not now.

Maybe not ever.

## 20

## BEAU

The Call is not for the faint-hearted. Neither is soaring high and almost coming in your pants at the sound of your girl climaxing under your touch, then straight afterward feeling her almost slipping away again as she tried to build that wall of hers back up again, brick by stubborn brick. Now, I'm not a young man, but fit and healthy as I am, I'm not sure my heart can take her telling me she's not ready again. Hearing those words...it hurt.

In some ways, I'm grateful to her for saying it too. It forced us to be raw and honest with each other for a change. The interaction had me more rattled and vulnerable than I think I've ever been. But the pure relief I now feel as we walk hand in hand back toward the firepit is nothing short of sheer perfection. This feels like moving forward.

And as much as I'd love to continue what we started behind the barn and have her in my bed tonight, I totally understand that there are the kids to think about in this relationship. So what we want is secondary to them. And by loving Molly, I'll also protect them as much, if not more than their sister because I believe in package deals and being honorable with one's intentions. Those kids need stability, certainty, and they need to know that this is the real deal between Molly and me before we make anything permanent. If that means taking the time to prove that to them and making the most of stolen moments behind barns, and weekends spent working around the ranch, then there are far worse things that could happen.

"Beau." Molly stops me just as we're about to round the corner of the ranch house. "I want to say sorry again for what just happened back there. I think I just had a bit of a moment where I freaked out. What we just shared, it was intense and I felt a little—"

"Off balance?"

"Yeah."

"Me too. That's how this Call thing has had me feeling ever since I realized we were meant to be together."

"When did you…" She looks down at our still-joined hands, a small smile tugging at her mouth.

"When did I know you were my One?"

"Yeah…"

"I've wanted you since that day I dragged Jesse into the Vet Clinic to ask the doc out." I squeeze her fingers and wait for her beautiful hazel eyes to lift back to mine. "Then I *knew* you were meant to be mine the day you came here to ream me out for paying for your truck."

Her head snaps up. "Seriously? I left and facepalmed because I thought I came across as rude and bull-headed."

"And gorgeous, and passionate, and sassy as hell. Yet proud, courageous, and not at all scared to put me in my place." Her eyes soften, and her grip on my hand tightens. "I meant what I said about a date, angel. There's no rush, though. I want you to be as sure as I am when it comes to you and me. I'll wait however long it takes. Besides, I figure we know this Call business is the real deal, what's the rush?"

"And I meant it when I said I don't want to wait any longer, Beau. Admittedly, it took me a while to realize that my attraction to you is more than just a little crush. But day by day, you've been there, chipping away little by little at my resistance, and you don't seem even a little bit daunted by my life status right now."

"That's because I'm not, angel. Not in the slightest. The kids are a part of you, and any man worthy of you needs to respect that they're your priority—as they should be. I'm proud of you and them. That doesn't mean I won't do whatever I can to make life a bit easier for y'all."

As expected, she opens her mouth to argue that point, but I stop her with a crushing kiss on her parted lips, taking the opportunity to glide my tongue into her mouth, working for that breathy whimper of hers until she grips my shoulders and her body melts into mine. *Fucking phenomenal.*

When we pull apart, we're both breathing heavy, and the very last thing I wanna do is let her go, but I can hear the kids mucking around with Miller and Sawyer and it's high time we got back out there.

"You good, angel?"

"Better than good, boss." The smile she gives me is so big and bright, I swear it warms me hotter than the sun on a summer's day. "Not sure I could feel any better, to be honest."

Unable to resist, I dip my head down. "More than ready to prove that theory wrong when I get you in my bed."

Her hitched breath is all the answer I need as I grab her hand again and move us toward the firepit.

"And so they return," Sawyer announces. "Did you get Buster's feed sorted out?" I frown, wondering what the fuck he's on about until he gives me a look that tells me I need to go along with him.

"You're back!" Cody says, running up to the two of us, Sage and Colson slowly coming up behind him. "Sawyer said you guys had to go see to Buster. Is he OK?"

"He's fine, buddy," I say, struggling to keep my expression neutral, especially when I can see Sawyer's smartass smirk from all the way over here.

"Buster needed feeding?" Jesse asks. "But I gave him some— Fuck, doc. What was that for?" Jesse rubs his ribs as he glares at Kendra and she shoots him the same 'go along with it!' look that Sawyer gave me. *Nice save, doc.*

To her credit, Molly just giggles against my arm and Ellie-Mae grins up at me and winks knowingly. "While you guys were gone, we suggested to the kids that they should ask you if it's OK to sleep over in the ranch house tonight. Saves you driving back home this late at night, especially on your birthday of all things."

"Oh," Molly says, shaking her head. "We wouldn't want to intrude."

"Never you mind about that, pet. We've got more rooms and beds than we know what to do with. It's no trouble."

"And Jesse and Miller said they'd take us out to the far edge of the ranch first thing in the morning," Cody says, turning puppy dog eyes to his sister. "*Please*, Molly. Can we? I'll be super good and do *all* my chores double fast when we get home. I promise." The kid sure knows how to present a good case, finishing off his speech by crossing his hand over his chest then holding out his little finger. "I'll even pinky promise."

"Hmm..." Molly rubs her chin, making a show of thinking it through. "What do you two think?" she asks, looking over at Sage and Colson.

Sage shrugs. "I *have* always wondered how far the ranch goes on."

Everyone looks to Colson, who puts his hand in the air. "Hey, you know I'd stay here any time just to learn more about ranching. But I'd rather we didn't have to drive home this late. I mean, it's not like we wouldn't be comin' back here tomorrow mornin' anyway, right?"

*Good fucking point, Cols.*

Molly turns back to Ellie. "Only if you're sure."

"Sure as a pig likes to roll around in the mud. Besides, more the merrier."

I let Molly go long enough for her to hook her pinky with Cody's and give the kids all a hug goodnight along with a murmured warning to be good and listen to Ellie-Mae before she steps back and Ellie turns to Cody.

"All right, kids. Let's get inside and see if I can raid Miller's hidden ice cream stash."

"Hey!" the man in question protests.

"Oh, husband, don't you worry. I'll buy you some more the next time I'm in town."

"You better," he grumbles, quickly shifting to smiling as soon as his wife leans over and smacks a kiss on his lips before leading the kids to the house.

With the kids now inside, everyone else seems ready to call it a night too, with Kendra and Jesse saying their goodbyes and moving to their quad bike to ride back to the Horse Haven next door. Sawyer heads for his truck and says he's got somewhere to be, while Randy heads for the ranch house with Miller, leaving Molly and me all alone.

"Well, they made themselves scarce fast, didn't they?" Molly giggles, her eyes shining brightly in the dim light of the dwindling fire. I close the distance between us and wrap my arms around her back, pulling her in close so she has to rest her hands on my chest and tip her head back to look at me.

"You wanna go stay in the ranch house too?" I say, my lips twisting up at the side.

"Is that where you sleep?"

"No. My room is in the bunkhouse."

"In that case, I have a *much* better idea."

I cock my head. "And what's that, angel?"

She wriggles out of my hold and slowly starts walking backward in the direction of the bunkhouse, a wicked grin on her face as she beckons me to follow. That glint in her eyes causes my cock to wake up and take notice of every step she takes. She looks me up and down, and her eyes flash with heat as they land on the bulge in my jeans.

Then she holds her hand out for mine. "How 'bout you follow me and find out... *boss*."

## 21

## MOLLY

He hooks an arm under my knees, the other wrapping around my shoulders as he lifts me and carries me from the bunkhouse door, making a beeline straight for a large bathroom, obviously having the same thought as I did that we should both clean up before getting dirty again.

The whole time, his lips are fused to mine, our tongues languidly caressing each other in a slow-burn kiss that's no less hot than the hard, hungry, desperate kisses we shared behind the barn. But now, there's no urgency. We have all night long, an opportunity I never expected—especially tonight. *Best birthday present ever!*

Once we're inside the surprisingly modern and clean bathroom, Beau slowly lowers me down to my feet, running his hands up my body, sending a shiver of anticipation searing through me. I may

not be a virgin, but this is—if I get my way—
about to be my first time with this man, and already, just the prospect of that means so much
more to me. And even if I didn't know about the
Call and the mountain lore, it would still be different. Because it's *him.*

"So damn beautiful," he murmurs, cradling my
face in his big hands and sweeping his thumbs
over my cheeks.

The side of my mouth lifts as I run my hands
around his back and glide them up, leaning my
chest against his "You're not too bad yourself."

"Glad you think so." He presses a soft and sweet
barely there kiss to my lips. "I thought you might
want to clean up before bed. I'll go grab you some
clothes and—" I shut him up by wrapping my
hand around the back of his head and tugging his
mouth to mine again, but I forgo soft and sweet
for deep, hard, long, and—I hope—reassuring. "I
thought we could shower together. It *is* my birthday, after all. Don't you wanna make this girl's
birthday dream come true," I rasp as I continue to
kiss along his jaw and down his neck.

"I didn't… I didn't wanna assume."

"We're alone, right?" He nods as he kicks his foot
against the door, shutting us in.

I step back and send him a saucy smirk before lifting my arms up and slowly undoing the buttons of my shirt. One by one, my eyes locked with the hooded hungry eyes of the heavy breathing cowboy in front of me.

Quirking a brow, I look him up and down and tip my head, hoping he'll follow the lead.

"You plannin' on seducing me, angel?"

"Well, I'd hope the seduction would be mutual. But I'm not opposed to using my womanly charms to persuade you."

He laughs against my lips, kissing me long and slow before stepping aside and reaching past me. As soon as he turns the water on, the room starts filling with steam. Then, seemingly satisfied that the water is warm enough, Beau walks me backward into the shower stall, turning his back to the water as his hands roam all over my wet slippery body as we take turns washing each other down.

Of course, I do the same, not about to miss out on my first opportunity to put my hands, fingers, lips, tongue over every part of his skin I can reach, every new sound and reaction I get from me encouraging my journey of discovery of a very naked, very sexy Beau Barnes. Every once and awhile he'll cup my jaw and tilt my chin up to kiss me, continuing to stoke the blazing wildfire burning inside me, the one he set alight.

I reach down and wrap my fingers around his thick erection, whimpering at the feel of soft skin covering hard steel, my eyes locked with his as I stroke up my hand up and down the shaft, his stuttered breaths and soft groans driving me on as I flex my grip and speed up, dragging the tips of my fingers over his heavy balls, learning, exploring, watching him closely for every single reaction. And boy, he does not disappoint. He cups his hand between my legs, grinding the heel of his palm against my clit, the attention not helping my concentration as the ache in my core soars and my need to do more, *have* more becomes overwhelming.

Not even realizing the water's been shut off, I barely have time to open my eyes when I'm lifted in his strong arms again, but this time there's no time to waste, and with not even a towel around his waist—or mine, for that matter—he stalks out of the bathroom and straight to the open door of the bedroom opposite, closing and locking the door behind us with one hand before moving to the bed. He puts a knee to the mattress, then lays me down on my back in front of him. Then he stays there, dragging his hungry gaze up and down my body, every nerve ending under my skin sparking to life under his inspection before I can't take any more. I jerk his mouth back to mine and wrap my legs around his back, my heels digging into the round mus-

cular globes of his ass as he rocks his hips
against me.

"Fuck, angel. You're too fuckin' much and not
enough. I want to take my time, but I need to
bury myself inside you so bad my cock aches with
it," he growls against my throat, swirling circles
over my skin with the tip of his tongue as he
drags his body down mine. Then his hand cups
my breast as he sucks my stiff peak between his
lips and draws me deep into his mouth, making
me buck off the bed like I'm at the rodeo.

"Ah. Oh god. Please," I beg, not caring how loud
or demanding I'm being. Beau is right. This is too
much and not enough all at once. My fingers grip
his shoulders, the sounds coming out of my
mouth unintelligible gibberish as he moves to the
other breast, paying it the same attention.

Beau's hum of satisfaction vibrates against my
nipple, sending a jolt of need straight between
my legs. He brings his mouth back to my lips,
diving his tongue back inside to tangle with
mine, while I pour every ounce of my desperation
into my movement, moaning against his lips as
he slides his shaft back and forth along my
soaked seam.

"Fuck. So damn wet for me," he says with a low
gravelly growl as he continues to thrust his body
hard against mine, pushing me into the mattress

as I squirm against him, unable to think of anything else but the feel of him, the taste of his lips against mine, and the growing ache inside me that only he can quell. His fingers tangle with my wet hair and pull my head back so he can run his lips up and down my throat, my pulse spiking with every scrape of his rough skin.

Bracing his hands on either side of my head, he surges up and looks down at me, my warm breath fanning over his skin as he dips his face so he's all that I can see. *He's all I wanna see too.*

"Feel what you do to me, angel."

"Please, Beau. I want to *feel* you." He rests his lips against mine, his pupils big and dark as they bore deep into mine.

"Where, angel. Tell me where you want me."

I grab his hand and guide it between us until his palm is cupping my sex, the slow gentle slide of his finger over my clit then down my seam making me shudder with pleasure.

His head drops to my shoulder with a guttural groan as he pushes first one, then two of his calloused fingers inside of me, my hips taking on a life of their own as they thrust up, urging him deeper. Beau lifts his eyes to meet mine, his gaze full of want and need, his voice hoarse and laced with lust.

All I can do is pant and moan, whimper and groan, his rumbling growls as I meet him thrust for thrust, stroke for stroke urging me on.

"I need you inside me. I'm about to explode. I want it all with you." My voice is hoarse, my need unmistakable as I punctuate my declaration with a rough, desperate, probing kiss. Beau's fingers speed up, his thumb rubbing over my clit as he presses his hips against my leg, letting me feel just how hard he is... how hard I've made him.

He smiles against my lips. "You feel so good. You doin' OK?" he murmurs, withdrawing and pressing in a little deeper.

I nod, incapable of words as my orgasm barrels straight at me like a stampede ready to trample me over. The moment he trails his tongue down my neck and rakes his teeth against the apex of my shoulder, I'm done for, my muscles tensing, my breath seizing, my heart pounding just before I cry out my release. "Beau! God! Yes!" I moan as wave after wave of the most exquisite, amazing, mind-blowing pleasure rolling over me again and again

"Fuck, I can't wait. Gotta feel you now, angel."

"Yes. Please," I whimper, spreading my legs wider as he fits his hips between my thighs, bracing himself on one arm as the other hand reaches down to notch the tip of his cock at my entrance.

Then, with his intense gaze locked with mine, he ever so slowly pushes himself inside me, inch by achingly delicious inch, until he's planted himself to the hilt, his pelvis tight against mine as he kisses my lips and licks his tongue into my willing mouth.

"Better than I ever fucking imagined it would be, Molly. You're fucking perfect."

I smooth my palms against his stubbled cheeks. "Well, so are you, so we must be perfect together then."

"Fuck yeah you are. Mine..." He draws his hips back. "All..." His eyes flash with heat and need and a possessive glare that's so hot I feel it right down to the tips of my toes. "Fucking mine." Then he drives into me, slamming his mouth to mine and swallowing my desperate moans with his rough grunts as no more words are spoken. I cling to him, wrapping my legs around him again, digging my heels into his butt cheeks, urging him to go harder and deeper into me until our thrusts become sporadic and uncontrolled.

My fingers return to his back, my nails pressing in, holding on as he continues to drive into me, over and over again, filling me with long hard, claiming strokes. Our kisses turn messy and rough, reckless and absolutely perfect, our tongues dueling as my hands roam everywhere I can reach.

Then I feel the pressure growing inside me, so big and monumental it should scare me, but I'm driven by this unbeknownst till now desperate burning need to get more, be more, to give both of us *more*. I never want this moment to end— even if the promised orgasm just about to hit me might just be the end of me.

With a final arch of my back, I clutch him tight and hold his mouth to mine, crying out into his mouth, my blood boiling, my skin feeling like I'm bursting at the seams as my orgasm detonates and I moan his name like the most reverent prayer. "Beau... *yes.*"

"Fuck, beautiful. Can't. Hold. On. Jesus. Yes. Fuck. *Angel!*" Beau stutters as he loses control and punctuates every word with a thrust of his hips before he drives his cock as deep inside me as he can go and gives himself over to the pleasure of *us*.

And as he rolls to his side and bundles my limp, spent body into his arms, only one thing is going through my mind.

*How soon can we do that again... and again?*

## 22

## BEAU

With a deep inhale, my senses are filled with the sweet scent of Molly still sleeping in my arms. She's got her face tucked into my neck like she's a little bird, and my heart fills to bursting knowing this gorgeous creature has chosen me. *I'm never going to let her regret giving into the Call for a moment.*

Pressing my lips against her temple, my grip around her tightens as I make a silent pledge to never let her go. She's mine. The mountain gave her to me, so that's really all there is to it. I'll work my fingers to the bone, bleed, sweat, and exhaust myself just to make sure she's looked after.

"Mmm," Molly hums, her body waking as she stretches out against me and presses tiny butterfly kisses against my pulse. "Good morning, boss."

"Mornin', angel." My voice comes out gruff as I hook a finger under her chin and tilt her head back so I can kiss her ruby red lips, swollen from a night full of feasting on each other's bodies. "Sleep OK?"

"Like a baby." She smiles and lifts an arm above her head, giving me the perfect view of her soft, lush breasts. I lean in and take her dusty pink nipple in my mouth, swirling my tongue until it peaks, and she arches against me. "Mmm, I like wakin' up with you as much as I like sharin' a bed with you, Beau Barnes."

"Well, I did promise I'd take care of you. And that includes *all* your needs." I move to the other breast, kissing and sucking as I glide my hand along the curve of her side before settling at her hip.

"And what about you? Who's gonna be takin' care of Beau?"

"This feels a lot like takin' care of me too, angel," I murmur as my hand shifts between her legs, seeking her wet center. A growl rumbles out of my chest when I find how soaked she is for me. Dipping down to her entrance, I start rhythmically fucking her with my fingers. "I'm never gonna get tired of feelin' how warm and tight you are every time I push in."

"Oh god. Yes. Yes. It's so good," she moans, writhing beneath me as I work her into a frenzy, my thumb on her clit while her hips lift and roll, fucking my hand right back as her features contort with beautiful pleasure.

My dick throbs with desire as her moans change to whimpers and she clenches around my fingers, almost strangling me until suddenly she releases and I feel her warmth pulse around me while I capture her cries in my mouth in a long, deep kiss. "Fuck, you're sexy when you come."

She smiles lazily as I roll my fingers in and out slowly to bring her down. "You have a way of bringing out the best in me," she says. "Which of course means, I need to repay the favor."

Placing her hand on my shoulder, she pushes lightly, but I catch her wrists, then pin both hands over her head as I stare into her eyes. "No tit for tat in this relationship, angel. I won't have it. You give what you want when you want it. I never want you actin' out of a sense of owin'. That ain't how this works."

"OK then. I *want* to suck your dick, boss. Desperately. Because the idea of tasting you the way you've tasted me turns me on."

"That's better," I say, grinning as I release her wrists and let her push me onto my back before she kisses her way down my body.

"You're right, it *is* better," she says, looking up at me as she kneels between my legs and takes my cock in hand. Stroking it languidly as she licks her lips, her gaze shifting to fixate on my length filling her palm. Then she releases a pleasurable hum before she flicks her tongue over my tip then swirls it around my girth, taking me deep in her mouth, moving up and down before she flattens her tongue against my base and takes me in as far as she can go.

"Fuck. Your mouth feels like heaven," I grunt, my hand sliding into her hair as she sucks hard and bobs her head up and down, bringing her hand into play with gentle pressure on my balls. Up and down, up and down. My eyes roll back and I hiss through my teeth, trying desperately not to thrust up or spill myself too soon. Because I don't wanna come in her mouth. No. The only place I want to unload is deep inside her body, where my seed belongs. "Sit on me, angel. I want in." My fingers flex against the back of her head as I pull her up and guide her back to my mouth, kissing her hard while I grab her by the thighs and position her on my lap, my cock pulsing against her seam.

"You know, boss. If this relationship is gonna work, you're gonna have to quit fightin' when I wanna do things for you," she says, sitting back and licking her lips while she trails her fingers down the center of my chest, moving to circle my nipples as she talks. "Because I *really*"—she rolls her hips against my hard length—"enjoy making you feel good too."

"I know. But you worry me, angel. You work so damn hard all the time, and all I wanna do is make your downtime as pleasurable and as easy as possible. Plus, I really like fucking you and making *you* come."

She leans in and presses soft kisses against my chest. "And I love that you treat me that way. It's so beautiful to feel cared for. But giving is in my nature. You've gotta let me give to you too. We're partners in this Call, after all. Aren't we?"

"Yeah. We're definitely partners."

"*Equal* partners?"

I grin as I reach up and take her face in both of my hands. "Not on your life." She moves to pull back, but I hold on tight, needing to make this point abundantly clear. "Angel, I'm gonna shower you with everything I can, everything I have for the rest of my days, and I'm never gonna say sorry for that. What's mine is yours and what's yours belongs to you and your siblings. I don't want any of that. I only want you. Just you. You hear me?"

"Yeah. I hear you, Beau. But—"

"But what? There's nothin' to argue about here, Molly, because this is all there is. You. Me. The kids. And the fact I love you so damn much my heart might actually catch fire from how much I need you."

She blinks rapidly as my words hit her. "You love me?"

"Yeah. With everything I have and then some," I whisper before I pull her in for a kiss that's filled with so much heat and longing I almost cry from it. And I haven't been brought to tears since I was just a kid. Loving her means that much to me.

"Oh, Beau," she whispers against my lips. "I love you too."

Flexing at the waist, I sit up and gather her in my arms, kissing her as we whisper sweet nothings to each other while she wraps her legs around my waist and I sink myself inside her body, my soul feeling complete once more. Then all our words stop as we replace them with nothing but feeling as we roll together, slow and gentle, then hard and fast until we're both crying out, coming together as our climax hits, and I spill myself into her quivering depths.

"Love you, Angel," I pant against her mouth, still holding her tight to me.

"I love you too, Beau," she says, and if those aren't the sweetest words in the English language. Then I don't know what is.

## 23

## MOLLY

I'm still walking on cloud nine later that afternoon, as Kendra and I are painting the porch of the ranch house at Horse Haven. Beau and Jesse have taken all of my siblings out with him again, Beau promising to bring them back before sundown in time for us all to get home and get ready for the school and work week ahead.

Last night and this morning were the stuff dreams are made of. Beau is so incredibly loving and attentive that my body is still singing from the pleasure he gave me—body and soul. I never knew falling in love could be this...this... *all-encompassing.* And now that I've had a taste, I don't ever want to go back to the scared and overly guarded person I was before. I'm glad I finally decided to let Beau in. And bonus—not only did I spend the night, and wake up in the arms of a wonderful, generous, *very* handsome man who's crazy about me. I get some alone time with my bestie too. *Twenty-four might just be my best birthday ever!*

"Ugh," Kendra says, standing up from her crouch and stepping back to admire the porch railing we've half-finished painting. "What do you think of this color?"

I move to my feet and move next to her. "It's pretty."

"Yeah... pretty. Not sure Jesse is gonna be a big fan of 'pretty'."

I nudge her with my shoulder. "Well, he's a big fan of *you*, and you're pretty."

"Pfft. You've gotta say that, you're my person."

"And would I lie to you about you being pretty?" I say with a questioning brow.

She turns and smirks at me. "Nope. But you *would* lie to me and say the color was pretty when really it looks like a big prickly—"

"Pineapple?" I tilt my head, as if changing my viewing angle will somehow miraculously stop Kendra's porch from looking like a pouffy lemon souffle or something.

"More like a yellow patch in the snow," she retorts, and I snort, fighting a giggle but losing the battle when Kendra looks at me and bursts out laughing.

"Oh, my god. It totally does," I cry, clutching my belly as we both shriek with laughter.

"Ugh. This is *so* not the look I was going for," she says once we calm down. "I want homely, welcoming, come and 'trust me with your traumatized horse', not 'I have no taste and decided to paint my house a garish *yellow*'. Jesse is *not* gonna like the fact we're going to have to repaint it... *again.*"

"What will this make it? The third time?"

She shakes her head and groans. "Shh. Don't remind me."

"OK. You know what this calls for?" I ask, bending down to place my paintbrush in the bucket of water to clean it.

"An intervention?" She smirks.

"How about a glass of wine from that bottle I spied in your fridge? Surely a paint color crisis deserves wine."

"I can't think of a better reason right now, not that we need one. Besides, how often do we get to just hang out and gab about things these days." She plops her brush in the bucket and then opens the screen door and leads me inside.

"Um… didn't we just have lunch last week."

"Yeahhh…" she replies.

"And then see each other at work every day."

While she retrieves the bottle of wine from the fridge, I sit down on one of the stools at the kitchen island and lean against the counter. "Uh-huh… what's your point, Molls? It's Sunday afternoon, I've just screwed up the porch *yet* again, and there're no husbands, soulmates, or kids around. What other reason do we need to drink wine?" As she says it, she's already filling two glasses and handing one over to me.

"God I love you, Kendie."

"Good. Because I love you too, which is exactly why you're gonna tell me what had you thinking so hard outside while you were paintin'. Because I swear I had to call your name four times before you realized I was talkin' to ya."

"Huh?" My cheeks heat up as she looks over at me with a knowing gaze and an equally curious smirk. "I take it you had a good sleepover in the bunkhouse last night?" She waggles her eyebrows, making me laugh.

"*May*be…"

"Maybe my butt. Going by those tired eyes of yours, I'm thinkin' there wasn't much sleeping going on. And more under than over."

"Kendra!" I gasp, but my best friend just grins at me.

"You're thinking of your cowboy, aren't you? Wondering when you might get another sleepover again."

I smile against the lip of my wineglass as I take a sip. "Of course. He's all kinds of wonderful."

"I knew he would be. Just like I knew you two would be great together. I'm so glad you're giving him a chance, Molls. He won't stop smiling, and I'm not sure I've ever seen you so…"

"Happy? Tired?"

"Deliriously exhausted." She holds up her glass in the air and clinks it against mine.

"So what are the benefits to having a best friend who's the Mountain's seer?"

"What do you wanna know?"

"It's just," I sigh, distracting myself by running the tip of my finger around the rim of the crystal. "I want this to work with Beau. Last night was wonderful and I really think we're moving forward toward something that could be amazing."

"But..." Kendra's expression is all business now. She's giving me her full attention and never have I been more grateful to have her by my side.

"How do I make this work? If Aster's books are anything to go by, this connection we have is going to last. But how do we work this out logistically? The kids, my jobs, Beau's responsibilities on the ranch and at the store..."

"Whoa there. Should we unpack all of that one by one or what?"

"I don't know!" I feel myself getting worked up and overwhelmed. "I just don't know what happens next. I can't see Beau moving away from the ranch, and I sure as hell won't be moving my whole family out of the only home they've ever known to live here. And even if I did, where would we even fit? The kids can't live in the bunkhouse, and we can't kick Randy out of the main house..."

"You finished? Or is there more?" she asks when I pause for a breath, her mouth tipping up on one side.

A huge sigh escapes me, my shoulders slumping under the weight of it. I look over at my best friend, begging her with my eyes for some kind of insight. Right now, I probably just need reassurance that I'm not losing my damn mind. "How do

I juggle everything I have right now while also adding Beau to the mix? I want a relationship with him so badly, but I'm afraid of throwing myself into this, then taking my eye off one of the ten balls I'm juggling. I'm barely able to keep them all in the air as it is."

She cocks her head. "Have you told Beau any of this?"

"I have," I say. "In a roundabout way, and he's made it clear that he knows I've got a lot going on and he just wants to be there for me and help."

"So let him."

My head jerks a little. "It doesn't work like that."

"Why not?" she says with a shrug.

"Because of the kids, the house, and me making sure I'm raisin' them right. All of that is *my* responsibility. I've never been one of those girls who was searchin' for someone to take care of things for me. I can't just dump it all in his lap and act like it's his responsibility too."

"But what if he wants it? You haven't asked him to take care of you. But I know he wants to make life easier for you in any way he can. So let him take care of you in the way you *need* him to. Talk it out, make it clear what you want and don't want out of this relationship. Be honest, don't be shy or embarrassed about anything. You lay it all out there and give him a chance to be honest right back. It's called communication. All the cool kids do it these days."

"Is it that easy, though? I mean, I'm stubborn, but Beau is somethin' else."

"It's called having a mature adult relationship. And the best part of it is, this isn't just a normal kind of relationship."

"Because of the Call?"

"Yes, but also because you've got me, and Jesse, and the rest of the Barnes family, and you've got one other special person standing in your corner cheering you on."

"Who's that?"

"The Mountain Spirit. She chose you for a reason, Molls. She may not make the journey an easy and seamless one, but there's always a reason for it. You've gotta trust the mountain to guide your heart, because as I've said before—"

"The Mountain Spirit doesn't get it wrong."

"Exactly. Look at me and Jesse, Ellie-Mae and Miller, and there's also Aster, your favorite author, and even the seer over at Bear Mountain Homestead, Gandalf. Even *he* has heard the Call —although from what I've heard, he had the easiest journey out of everyone."

"How did he get so lucky?"

"Only the spirit knows, and She's rather choosy as to who gets the Call and when, remember? So he must've earned an easy journey."

"Is there such a thing as an easy journey when it comes to the Call?"

"I dunno. But it certainly helps to know that in the end, you have the love of a man who completes you in every single way and you do the same for him. It's an amazing feeling, Molly. I promise, when you're old and gray and looking back on all of this, you'll do it with a smile knowing it led you to a life filled with love."

"Well, that's one thing I can count on I suppose."

"It is, I promise."

"And there's something else I can *definitely* count on."

"What's that?"

"At least Beau will be my silver fox, eventually."

"You and your romance books."

"Hey! Don't knock it till you've tried a few more of them."

"I have, remember. I read all of Aster's ones."

"Yeah, and there are so many more. But believe me, Silver foxes are *hot*."

"Just like cowboys," Kendra adds with a knowing wink

I lift my glass back in the air for a toast. "Now *that*'s something to drink to."

"Are you gonna be our dad now?" Cody asks as we take a slow walk on horseback around the perimeter of the ranch, the purpose of which is to show the kids how big the property is and to check the fence line while we're at it. I have Jesse and Sawyer along for the ride, and it's been a great learning experience for Colson who's already had to repair a snapped wire from a fallen tree branch. The kid's on cloud nine. If I didn't know he was a Roberts, I'd swear he was like a long-lost Barnes brother.

"Why would you think that?" I ask the kid with a laugh, pulling my horse, Max, back in line with Cody who's riding Buster—Spencer chose to stay at Horse Haven today, when we left him he was too busy dozing in the sunshine to even lift his head our way.

"'Cause you're around a lot. And you teach us stuff. You know, like a dad does. Our dad used to do stuff like that too."

"I see," I say, nodding at his reasoning and seeing how he drew that conclusion.

"He can't be our *dad,* Cody," Colson pipes up. "Even if it *was* possible, it'd make him Molly's dad too since she's our sister, and that would just be weird." Sawyer snorts and Jesse starts choking with laughter, something he morphs into a cough when my narrowed gaze lands on both of them.

"Yeah, but Molly's more like our mom than our sister," Cody continues. "And if Beau was our dad, then we could live on the ranch and feed the cows and the goats every day. I'd really like that."

"It doesn't work like that, Cody," Colson reprimands. "You've got your head in the clouds."

"Let the boy dream," Sage throws in. "I don't blame him for wishin' he could be here all the time. Certainly beats bein' cooped up at home while Molly works a thousand jobs."

"There's nothin' wrong with our house," Colson says over his shoulder, scowling at Sage. "It's where we grew up, and Molly's only workin' so hard to keep us all together. Did you want to end up in the system?"

"Of course I didn't," Sage says with a serene smile. "And I love Molly for everything she's given up for us. But if her bein' with Beau means we get to come out here more often and maybe she works a little less and we can *see* her more, then I'm all for that—no pressure on you, Beau."

"I'm not pressured," I say, flashing her a grin. "I'm in this with your sister for the long haul, I think y'all should know that. As for becomin' your dad, Colson is right, that's not gonna happen. But I am here to be your friend and to help you guys any way I can. Molly is super important to me, and as a result, you kids are all important to me too."

"So we *can* come and stay?" Cody asks, a bright light in his eyes.

"That's not my decision to make, bud. That's for Molly and you three to decide on your own. I'm not gonna push you guys to leave your home or anythin'." I meet Colson's eyes then, and he gives me a single, grateful nod. Something I return, because he needs to know that I respect the fact that me coming into their lives, while intended to help, can present challenges too. I don't want to add to their woes.

"What's that over there?" Sage asks after we've rounded the western edge of the property and started heading back toward home. "The buildin'." She points and squints off into the distance.

"Oh, that's probably somethin' for another time," I say, being mindful that Colson probably doesn't want to see what that is after the conversation we just had.

But at exactly the same time, Jesse says, "That's Beau's cabin."

"You're building a cabin?" Sage asks with a gasp. "What for?"

"It's nowhere near ready," I say. "So it's not somethin' we need to worry about right now."

"Is it for you to live in?" Cody asks.

"Well, yeah," I say, rubbing the back of my neck. "Can't live in a bunkhouse forever, right?" I look over at the skeleton of a cabin my brothers and I started building for me a few months ago. The goal was to have it ready by the time I heard the Call, but the Call came my way sooner than any of us expected. So even if Molly and the kids *were* ready to move to the ranch, I couldn't exactly accommodate them right now. And I think that's for the best. The key to solidifying our relationship as a unit is to take this slow and steady. A bit like this cabin really—start with a strong solid foundation and then slowly build it up. I wanna prove to Colson, especially, that his sister is it for me, and that can only be done by turning up and being there, proving he can trust me to look after his sister and his family. All of which I have every intention of doing—however long that may take.

"I wouldn't mind livin' in a bunkhouse forever," Colson says, earning himself a nod of camaraderie from Sawyer.

"Hells yeah. Big benefits only dealin' with one room and a communal livin' area," he adds. "You should see how busy that place gets durin' calvin' and harvestin' times. Our cousins come in and we hire out a few more ranch hands, and it's like a party house. I, for one, love it."

Colson beams. "Hope I can put *my* hand up for ranch hand duty," he says, one eye on me.

"When you're finished school," I say over my shoulder. "Then I'm all for talking it over with your sister." It's like I can feel his scowl. But at the same time, I know Molly's stance on this, and I'm not gonna promise something I can't deliver on.

"I'll be eighteen by the time I finish school. So it'll be my choice to make," he shoots back.

"He's got you there," Sawyer says.

"Yeah. He does," I admit, my focus on Colson. "But, Cols, your sister has been fightin' tooth and nail to make sure you have the chance to get a college education the way she didn't. So at the very least, you need to seriously consider if ranchin' really is what you want, or if it's just the easiest thing you can think of."

"Ain't nothin' easy 'bout ranchin'," Jesse puts in.

"I know that already," Colson says.

"OK. But you've still got some time to think about it, right?" I continue. "Maybe give it a month or two, think on it long and hard and then you need to sit your sister down and have a conversation."

"And what if she won't listen?"

"Well, if you work hard and keep your grades up, prove you've got the work ethic of a man who wants to put his all into this land, then I'll have your back."

"Care to shake on that?" Colson quirks his brow and rides over next to me, holding out his hand.

"Kid knows what he wants," Sawyer says.

"He's not a kid," I say at the same time as Colson mutters, "I'm not a kid."

Which just makes Sawyer's smirk widen and Jesse laugh under his breath.

"I give you my word," I say, giving Colson's hand a firm squeeze. "Graduate and keep out of trouble, and if you can get Molly on board, there'll be a job for you workin' the land here with me."

His eyes bore into mine, as if he's trying to get a read on me. When he nods and moves away again, I realize he must've seen whatever he was looking for.

Cody giggles. "He sure sounds like a dad."

"Not our dad," Colson grumbles, at which point Sawyer suggests we pick up the pace a little so we don't miss dinner.

You can say a lot about Sawyer, but the man knows how to read a room well. I canter after him gratefully, knowing that I made ground with Colson today, but that doesn't mean the work is done. He loves this ranch as much as those of us who were born and bred here, but he also loves his family. And I don't wanna be the guy who messes with that. I've got a fine line to walk along, here.

## 25

## MOLLY

The following Thursday, after my birthday and the wonderful sleepover with Beau, I'm still buzzing—physically and figuratively. Since Sunday, Beau and I have seen each other every day. Whether it be at the supply store, or him bringing me lunch at the Vet clinic, and then him and Sawyer hanging out at the Lair during my shift last night—Sawyer loving all the attention he was getting on the dance floor while Beau and I only had eyes for one another.

I still get the tingles whenever he's near, and when we touch, it's like I wanna crawl out of my skin and crawl all over him—true story. My stomach flips at the thought of him, my heart pounds whenever I see him, and I can't help blushing whenever I remember our lovemaking.

The intensity of my feelings for the man is still overwhelming, but that's understandable. I mean, it's not like the Mountain Spirit just chose any ol' girl to be Beau Barnes's soulmate. She chose me. So I'm doing what I promised Beau I'd do, I'm believing in us... in our feelings for each other, in the way he makes me feel, and the way he shows it in his words and his actions.

But it's high time I sat down with the kids and made sure that *they* are all feeling OK about me seeing Beau. Which is why I've made two big bowls of popcorn for an impromptu family movie night—Cody's choice, which means we're getting ready to watch the Cowboys & Aliens movie.

I take a seat next to Sage and, with a deep fortifying breath, decide it's now or never.

"Before we get started, could I have a quick talk to you all about something?" I ask, looking between the three of them and *not* missing the smirk Colson sends Sage. Narrowing my eyes at my sister, she doesn't even try to look surprised when she meets my eyes again. "Wait. What was that about?"

"What was what?" She tries to feign innocence, but I know better. I switch my attention to my brother.

"Cols?" I ask.

"Nothin', Molls. What did you wanna talk about?"

"Well... I guess I just wanted to check in with you guys about things."

"Things?" Cody says, scrunching his nose up. "Like what?"

"Yeaaah, Molly. Like what?" Sage sing-songs, her gaze full of amusement at my obvious discomfort. I shake my head at her, not missing the snort coming from Colson's chair either. *Was I this annoying as a teenager?*

"Right. Let's just rip the bandage off. Beau and I are seeing each other... Romantically."

Cody releases a loud relieved sigh. "Well, *duh*. We see Beau every weekend."

Colson chuckles and hooks an arm around Cody's neck, giving him a noogie. "Bud, she means they're datin'."

Cody's frowns. "Wait... I already knew that."

That makes my brows lift sky high. "Yeah? When did you get so smart?"

"I'm eleven, Molly. I know a bit about love and stuff."

I can't help but laugh at how candid he is. "OK. And are all of you cool with that?"

"I am," Cody says. "Beau's really cool, and the ranch is *awesome*. And I like seeing you happy too. You smile more now."

"Yeah? I *feel* happier now," I say thickly, scrubbing him on the head before I turn to the others. "What about you two?"

Cols leans forward with his elbows on his knees and a smirk on his face. "Honestly, Molls, I was startin' to wonder what was wrong with you two."

"In what way?"

"I guess what he *means* is: what took you guys so long?" Sage butts in. "It's been obvious this whole time that he has a soft spot for you, and you haven't exactly been discreet with the way you look at him either. You're all heart eyes and goofy grins whenever you think no one is looking. Actually, you're so head over heels for the guy that you don't even notice when someone *is* lookin'."

Cody giggles and clutches his hands against his chest while he flutters his lashes. "She's all, 'Oh Beau, you're so dreamy and handsome'." The other two laugh, and I feel my cheeks turn scarlet.

"Really? I'm not *that* bad."

"Yeah, you are, Molls," Sage confirms. "Besides, it's not like you were sleepin' in the ranch house with us the other night either."

I bury my face in my hands, hiding my bright red cheeks. "Ohmigod."

"Where did she sleep then?" Cody asks, as innocent as my eleven-year-old brother should be.

"She had a sleepover too, bud. Might have another one again in future. You're cool with that, right?" Colson says.

"Yeah. Sleepovers are great fun! You can jump on beds, and have pillow fights..." Cody runs through his very innocent list while my brain makes it very adult and I try not to choke.

I peek out through my spread fingers to see Colson smirking up a storm as he continues. "Agree with you there. And just think, if Beau is Molly's boyfriend, that means we get to spend *heaps* of time at the ranch."

"Wicked! But we can still live here, right? Because Cols said—"

"Forget what I said. I'm just happy Molly has found someone who wants to treat her right. Beau is a good guy. I'm happy for her."

"Definitely happy for you, Molls," Sage says, smiling at me as she leans over and gives my leg a squeeze. "Especially because I know you wouldn't risk your heart or sit us down like this unless it was serious. And something tells me that Beau is *more* than serious about you. In fact, I think he's as serious as it gets." *Yeah. I know he is too. Lucky for me, I'm just as certain as well.*

"There's a little more to it. Something kind of...magical."

"Is this about the mountain?" Sage asks, piquing my interest. *Say what now?*

"Ok. Now you're freaking me out. How do *you* know about the mountain?"

Cody and Colson lean forward in their seats, looking puzzled. To her credit, Sage doesn't shy away or lie. "Well, I wanted to know what was so good about those mountain man books you read, so I *may* have started readin' them."

"And... what did you think of them?"

It's my sister's turn to blush this time. "They're really good. A little steamy, but I like the story-tellin' and how each couple has their own unique journey toward bein' together."

"Yeah. That's what I like too," I say, my heart swelling at this rare moment of female bonding with my sister over books of all things.

"It also helps that the men sound really hunky and dreamy," she says with a wistful look in her eyes.

Colson starts making gagging noises, earning a frown from me and the middle finger from our sister.

"*Sage!* Don't flip the bird to your brother."

"He deserved it."

"Even if he did, don't do it in front of Cody."

Cody rolls his eyes. "It's *just* the middle finger, Molls. It's not like she told him to fu—f*udge* off like she did the other day."

I purse my lips together, trying hard to keep a straight face. But I'm only so strong, so when Sage's mouth twitches and Colson smirks, I lose the fight and just start laughing.

"All right. Back to the mountain. What's so special about it? What are you and Sage going on about?" Colson asks.

"Well... there's a belief that the mountains along the same range as Eagle are home to a Mountain Spirit that looks after the protectors of the land— like the Barnes family and Miller's brothers back on Bear Mountain—and the Lore is that the Mountain Spirit rewards its protectors by calling their soulmates to the mountain."

"Hang on... you're saying that on the mountain —*our* mountain—there's a Mountain Spirit that decides who gets to meet their soulmate?" Colson asks. His tone isn't skeptical or disbelieving. He seems intrigued.

"Yep."

"And did the mountain call you?" Cody continues. "Like on the phone? Or was it like yelled from the mountain top, like a yodel?"

"There isn't like some little man running around the top of the hill wearing a green suit and yodeling with goats running around, Cody," Sage says.

"Well, how am I to know that?" he retorts. "What is it then?"

"So, it's really hard to describe. But it's more like a feeling so strong that you're kind of *drawn* to your soulmate." Realizing I have all of their attention, watching the movie seems to be the last thing on their minds. "Wait, you guys really wanna know about this?"

"Hell yeah. Sage, pass me the snacks. Who needs movies about cowboys and aliens when we've got our own real-life story about cowboys and the Mountain Spirit acting as their wing-woman to hear about," Colson says, taking a bowl of popcorn from our sister. "Besides, if I end up working the ranch, maybe this Lore will move on to me."

"Lord knows, you need all the help you can get when it comes to women," Sage mutters, calling out a "hey!" When a piece of popcorn hits her head and Colson and Cody high-five each other.

That's how we end up spending our evening. Me, my sister, and our two brothers, sitting around the living room, talking about everything I've learned about the Mountain's Call. And by the time we say goodnight and head off to our beds, I realize how truly blessed I am. Because not only do I have a good man in my life, I have the best siblings a girl could ask for. And going by the way they reacted to not only my news tonight, but my crazy, almost unbelievable story about a *Mountain Spirit* bringing me and Beau together, I definitely think I'm raising them right.

Now, I just have to see how this new acceptance of my dating Beau works out. Because if my current feelings toward him are anything to go by, this relationship isn't slowing down any time soon. There are some big decisions to be made in the future, and we're all going to have to make them together.

## 26

## BEAU

"If you hold this drywall in position, I'll run the nail gun along the edges to secure it, then Sawyer can follow after us, doing a more thorough job attaching it to the studs and blocking. Then we'll just keep repeating that process until we're done. Got it?" Miller says, looking between Sawyer and I as we stand in the hollowed-out room that will eventually become my cabin's living area.

In the month since Molly and I started officially dating each other, my brothers and I have made a lot of progress on the shell the kids originally saw. We've put plywood on all the outer walls, had the wiring and pipes fitted, and now we're at the point where we're finishing the walls before all the fixtures can go in. It's amazing what can be accomplished when you're motivated by the words of a young boy.

Ever since we took that ride around the perimeter of our land, and Cody mentioned how he wanted to be able to wake up on the ranch more often—Sage too, for that matter—I've been driven to get this place finished as soon as possible. Not because I want them all to leave their family home and come live with me right away, but to give them their own space for when they do come and stay on the ranch. Currently, they're all still bunking down at the ranch house each weekend, while Molly and I stay in the bunkhouse, and that isn't really ideal, nor is it fair on Randy who's the only one living in the main house these days. So, whether it's for a weekend, a week, or longer, I want them all to have their own bed and private rooms. I want them to see with their own eyes that there'll always be space for them here no matter which road Molly's and my relationship takes in the future, whether it's kids or just marriage—hopefully both.

Colson, of course, may not want a room in the cabin. He's growing into a man, so he probably wants his own space too. So depending on how he reacts when I show them all this place, maybe I'll chat to Molly about letting him test out life in the bunkhouse. He hasn't come to a solid decision over college versus ranching yet, so I think it might be good for him to take that deep dive into the lifestyle and see if it gels with him as much as he thinks it will. As Jesse pointed out, nothing about ranching is easy.

"All I'm hearin' is that I get to wield the nail gun." Sawyer lifts the tool from his side and squints one eye, making *pew-pew* noises like a little kid. "So, I'm good with that."

"Hey, careful where you point that thing," Miller says, stepping out of harm's way.

"I'm not gonna shoot ya with it."

"Not intentionally. But, it fuckin' hurts when one of those things gets ya, believe me. My twin, Mason, and I were fuckin' around with them when we first bought some for our carpentry business, and I ended up copping a nail to the thigh. A trip to emergency and a tetanus shot later, and we learned to quit playin' Star Wars with tools."

"Decided to stick with finger guns from there on out?" I tease, holding my thumb and forefinger out and making an explosive noise as I aim off into the distance.

"Yeah. Offcuts of wood work too," Miller says with more seriousness than I expected, causing me to grin as I select a piece of drywall off the stack.

"How unfun," Sawyer says, with a down-turned mouth as he lowers the nail gun and sighs. "At least actually nailing shit with them is still fun."

"Oh yeah," Miller says, lifting his gun once I've positioned the drywall against the studs. "I've been a carpenter for years, and these things never get old." He places the gun and sets it off three times on each side of the drywall before he blows over the end of it.

Sawyer chuckles then goes to town, securing the board properly. I get the next sheet and continue the process.

"Saw the posters up in town about the rodeo comin' at the end of Summer," I say to Sawyer as we work. "You all signed up?"

"Sure am," he says, tongue poking out of his mouth as nails the wall rhythmically. "Wouldn't miss it."

"Aren't you worried you're gonna throw your back out doing that shit?" Miller asks. "I mean, you're not exactly a spring chicken anymore."

"We can't all be little babies playin' at bein' a man like you, young Miller," Sawyer teases our thirty-five-year-old brother-in-law. As the youngest, and being married to Ellie, who's even younger at twenty-four, we love to give him shit about being a baby cowboy-in-training.

"Being the man Ellie-Mae needs isn't about playin' for a minute. I'm her husband. I'm the father of her child. And I'm the man she leans on when she needs holdin' up. It's just how this works. Right, Beau?"

"Sure is," I say, selecting the next piece of drywall. "Life is just different now that I have Molly and the kids in my life. Before, I'd do whatever pleased myself once all the work was done. But now, my first thought is always for them. How can I make that girl smile? How can I make the kids' day better?" I shrug as I lift the board to the wall. "It's just how it is when the Call joins you to your soulmate."

"Sounds hideously suffocating," Sawyer says over the *ka-chung* sound of each nail going in. "The more you guys talk about it, the more I hope the Call *never* comes my way."

Miller and I look at each other and smile, but we leave it at that. Sawyer's time will come when it comes, and only then will he see. *But by god is it gonna be fun to watch him fall on his bachelor sword.*

"You told Molly about this place yet?" Miller asks, his attention moving to me.

"Nah. Plan is to surprise her with it when it's done. One of her worries about us bein' together is wonderin' how we're supposed to blend our lives. So I reckon she's gonna love seeing that I've built a home for her—for all of us—with my bare hands."

"Not just *your* fuckin' hands," Sawyer says, waggling his fingers at me as he activates the nail gun with the other and slips, the nail shooting into the flooring and landing right beside his foot. He breathes out slowly as he stares down at it. "Holy shit!"

Miller reaches out and takes the power tool from Sawyer's hand. "Ah...Maybe Beau should take over the nailing from here."

"Yeah..." he says, sounding more than a little rattled.

Maybe the Call isn't the only thing that'll shake my brother up. Seems like a good ol' power tool can sometimes do the trick too.

## 27

## MOLLY

There are many things I'm thankful to Beau for. He's kind, supportive, thoughtful, looks damn good in a pair of jeans, wears a cowboy hat like a romance cover model, and kisses me like it's his favorite thing to do. But after a wonderful afternoon at the Eagle Mountain Spa with Ellie-Mae, Kendra, and Sage while he and the boys do some 'manly work'—as they said—back on the ranch, there's no way I'm not going to be showering my man with all kinds of affection and loving once I get back.

I feel like a new woman. All from being cleaned, slathered in all types of smelly colorful goo, exfoliated, massaged, and steamed. It was my first time but there's no way I wouldn't work ten jobs to make sure I can treat myself again in future. But I don't even have to do that anymore since Ellie-Mae and Beau asked if I'd like to take on a more permanent role working at the Supply store. The better hours and pay meant I could give up working at the Lair. And let me tell you, having my nights free again is a holiday in itself.

After eating a wonderful lunch in Timber Falls, we head back to Kinleyville, still buzzing from our day of bliss when we walk into the ranch house.

"Oh hey, y'all. What's happenin'?" Ellie asks as she walks through the kitchen to where *all* the guys are gathered. The air feels stilted somewhat, thick with something that feels a lot like dread. I want to shake it off because it sticks to my skin like memories I don't even want to think about, but my stomach drops the minute I step around Ellie-Mae and my gaze falls on a prone Colson lying on the couch with a bandage on his wrist, a cut on his temple, and an ice pack being held to his head.

"Ohmigod!" I cry, crossing the room so fast I swear my feet barely touch the ground. "Cols." My voice breaks as I take him in. He winces when he shakes his head at me.

"I'm fine," he grunts, which just earns him narrowed eyes.

I stand there looking him over, hands on my hips and my brain getting ready to explode. *I leave for one damn day and look what happens!* "Explain."

"What happened, Cols?" Sage asks, sidling up to me. "You lose a fight with a horse or something?"

"Nah. More like a Gator tried to do a death roll when I turned a corner."

*"What?"* I gasp, my eyes snapping to where Beau is leaning in the doorway, his expression serious.

"Angel, it was an accident. He took a corner too fast and flipped over. He was in a roll cage and belted in place. So he's gonna be fine. We called a cousin of Ellie's who's a doctor, and apart from being a bit banged up, Colson is gonna be fine."

"Fine? *Fine?* Does he *look* fine?"

"I *can* talk, you know," Colson says, swinging his legs over the side of the couch and sitting up, definitely looking a little worse for wear. My anger, worry, and fear hit me like a freight train all at once.

"Sore wrist and probably a mild concussion, Mols. Nothing worse than I'd get on the football field. A good night's sleep and some Tylenol is all I need."

"What you need is damn bubble wrap!"

Randy and Jesse chuckle at that, but stop when my scathing glare cuts their way.

"Where's Cody?"

"Mucking around in the barn with Sawyer and the horses. He's fine," Beau replies, pushing off the door and moving my way. "Angel, they're fine."

That's when I snap. "They're not fine! Colson is hurt and I'm..." I look down at myself, feeling sick that I just spent my entire day focused on myself when I should have been here making sure my siblings weren't trying to kill themselves on farm equipment.

"Molly, it's OK. We're all OK," Sage murmurs, slipping an arm around my waist. I shrug her off and step back, holding my hands up because I can't deal right now. *I should have been here.*

"No. No. This shouldn't be happening. I shouldn't have left." I touch my hand to my forehead. "I need to check on Cody."

"He's with Sawyer," Beau says. "He's OK."

"Stop saying that everything is OK. I let my guard down for one moment and take one day for myself, and *this* is what happens?" I gesture to Colson on the couch.

"Angel."

"I *knew* this was too good to be true. I just *knew* it. Life is never this good. This perfect," I mutter to myself as my chest tightens and images of being at the hospital with my dad, with my mom, go flashing in my mind, reminding me of what could've happened—another loss, another funeral. *I can't go through that again.*

This is my fault. All because I wasn't here. I was off gallivanting around at a *day* spa getting scrubbed and rubbed instead of looking after *my* kids. Who does that? I'm a pseudo-parent. I have responsibilities. And apparently, the universe decided to have one hell of a time and remind me of that.

I turn to Kendra. "Did you *see* this happening? Is this another thing that you knew would happen but you *couldn't* tell me? What *lesson* is this supposed to teach me, huh?'

Her eyes flash wide before gentling, and that cuts me deep. She shakes her head, but I don't know whether this is her not knowing, or not telling me because of whatever stupid Seer rules she abides by.

"Angel…" Beau's soft, soothing voice doesn't have the desired effect. All I can think is I need to get away from here. From the mountain, from the ranch, from everything. I need to take the kids, hop in the truck, and go back to our lives where there's no damn farm machinery or animals or anything that could hurt my family. *I'm not losing anyone else.*

"I've gotta go... I've gotta..." My body moves before I even know what's happening, and then I'm running, my legs pumping as fast as they can go.

"Molly, wait!" Beau calls out. But I'm too far gone, pushing through the ranch house door and outside.

"Give her a minute, Beau," I hear Kendra say just before I turn and run behind the bunkhouse, not even thinking about where I'm going or what I'm doing. I pass the barn and don't stop. Cody's yelled, 'Hey Molly,' fading into the distance.

Then, as wild as it seems, it's as if my mind clears, giving me a brief moment of peace amongst the chaos of my swirling emotions. It's like there's a voice inside of me, *in* my head. A soft, soothing, almost ethereal tone that instantly has my body relaxing, my mind clearing and my pulse slowing down back to normal.

*Come to paradise. Come to see me, and I'll show you the way...*

It's not until I run through trees and come across the beautiful waterfall Beau brought us all to one weekend that the voice in my head makes sense.

*Talk to me*, she says. *And everything will turn out just the way it was always meant to be.*

So, sitting on a rock overhanging a steaming hot spring, next to the most beautiful waterfall I've ever seen, I start talking to what I'm guessing is the Spirit of the Mountain.

And I can only hope that she hears me like I can hear her.

## 28

## BEAU

"**M**olly!" I circle around the buildings, calling out her name and wondering where the hell she could've gone. Back when we were kids, games of hide and seek could go on for hours because the ranch has so many nooks and crannies. That means if she doesn't wanna be found, I could be searching for hours. "Molly!"

"Lost somethin'?" Sawyer asks from where he's casually leaning against the barn door without his boots on. I look down and frown. There's just a pair of socks on his feet with a hole in them where his big toe is poking out.

"Looks like I'm not the only one. Where the hell are your shoes?"

"Cody's got 'em on. He's tryna prove he's a real cowboy by spinning a lasso over his head. He's been at it a while, but I haven't got the heart to tell 'im the rope he's usin' is too floppy." Sawyer grins, and I look past him into the barn. Sure enough, Cody is there with one of the soft ropes we sometimes use to tie bridles, trying to spin it over his head.

"He's tenacious. I'll give 'im that," I say, chuckling slightly because the kid looks comical in Sawyer's big boots and hat.

"He reckons he's gonna be in the rodeo when he's older like me. Figured I should take 'im under my wing."

"Have fun fightin' Molly over that one. She just took off upset over Colson rollin' the Gator earlier, so I can't see her reactin' well to her eleven-year-old brother wantin' to learn bull ridin'.""

"If it's in his heart, he'll go for it, anyway," Sawyer points out, wise despite everything else about him.

"I guess that's the only way to live life, huh? Followin' your heart?"

He nods. "And yours just ran that way." He points across the field where we normally keep the heifers leading up to the breeding period, but now it stands empty so the soil can rejuvenate and the grass can regrow.

"Thanks," I say, immediately turning to follow after her.

"Tell her she raised some cool kids," he calls after me, making me smile despite my worry for Molly's state of being right now.

"I will."

"Beau!" I'm only a few yards past the gate when Kendra comes running after me. "I know where she is."

"Let me guess? Paradise Springs?" I say, as she slows her step and walks alongside me.

"Dammit! Do you mean I didn't even need to run that fast?" she says, panting and clutching her side.

"It's the best place to think in the direction Sawyer pointed. So call it an educated guess. It's where I'd go in her shoes."

"OK." She nods and keeps walking alongside me for a second. "You know she doesn't blame you, right? She just...she had a bit of a panic attack. She's lost so much in such a short time, and even though she puts on this strong and resilient facade, she's really just clinging desperately to everything she has left. Seeing Colson hurt rattled her. Maybe even brought back memories of her parents, you know?"

"Yeah," I say, feeling nothing but empathy for all the Roberts kids. I was never just battling Molly's pride. I was battling her fear of getting hurt again, too. Losing your parents at any age is tough, but having it happen when you're so young is a hardship I don't wish on anyone. "I know she's fragile, Kendra. It's why I've been treadin' so careful with her. If this were up to me, they'd be pickin' out paint colors and packing up to move to the ranch to live with all of us out here. But it's not up to me at all."

"Grief is a powerful thing. It ebbs and flows like the rivers. Most of the time, it meanders about at a normal pace that we can handle. But sometimes it rains so much the banks burst, and we don't know what to do with all that water."

"Guess Molly's response to that is runnin', huh?"

Kendra smiles as we reach the other side of the paddock and stop. "This time. But something tells me that next time, it's you she'll be running to."

A gentle smile takes over my face. "That somethin' you saw, or somethin' you're just sayin' to make me feel better?"

Kendra taps her nose. "We'll just have to wait and see."

## 29

## MOLLY

I sense him before I even turn my head. That's the Call for you though, you feel the other half of your soul whenever they're near.

Looking over my shoulder, I watch as a relieved, gentle-gazed Beau crosses the clearing and walks toward me. There's a wariness in his expression, not at all like the annoyance I thought I might see after the way I freaked out earlier.

"Hey," I whisper as he takes a seat on the rock next to me. I hold my arm out, sighing with relief when he covers my hand and laces his fingers with mine. "How'd you find me?"

"Might've had a bit of guidance from the mountain's resident Seer."

I nod because of *course* Kendra would know where I might've ended up. Hell, *I* didn't have a clue until I got here, then again, I had a little guidance of my own.

"I kinda felt you, too. What made you run all the way out here?" he asks, rubbing his thumb back and forth over my skin.

"If I told you there was like this little voice in my head, you'll probably think I'm crazy." I shrug, my eyes focused on the soothing feel of his hand in mine.

"Try me, angel. It's not like I'm not aware of the magical powers this mountain has." He lifts my arm and brushes his lips ever so gently against my knuckles. "She brought me you, after all. And for that, I owe her gratitude."

My heart skips a beat and warmth washes over me. "She did. She also made sure you never gave up on me." I sweep my eyes up to his. "Even now, after I lost it and went a little crazy back there."

Beau's mouth tugs up on the side, and a dimple pops out. "Maybe you freaked out a *little*, but I think it's understandable. You've suffered through a lot of loss. We should've thought to call and tell you what had happened so you didn't get blindsided when you came home."

*Home.*

"Might've avoided my tantrum back there and an unexpected walk up the mountain."

He smirks, looking so damn handsome he takes my breath away. *I'm totally head over heels for this man.* "I dunno. It was a nice day for a long walk, and I kind of like being up here with you. It's like we're in our own little—"

"Paradise."

He squeezes my hand. "Exactly."

"I'm still sorry for reacting the way I did."

"Yeah? Well, I'm sorry Colson got hurt. And I take full responsibility for it. I thought he'd be fine because he's proven himself to be trustworthy and responsible, but he's still young, and I have to remember that."

"Why was he driving the Gator on his own, anyway?"

"We were finishin' off a buildin' project on the western edge of the ranch, and we needed something that was back at the barn. He put his hand up to go get it. And since it was the quickest, easiest solution, I agreed. He's just taken to ranch work like a duck takes to water, and I wanted to build his confidence up because I think he knows what he wants, but he's too afraid to say it out loud and really make a go of it."

"He wants to come and work on the ranch when he graduates, doesn't he? He doesn't wanna do college at all?"

"Angel," he says with a heavy sigh. "That's not a conversation for you and me to have. It's something you need to talk about together. But I'm serious when I say there's a job here for him when he wants it—no matter what you both decide." I open my mouth but he continues, his expression turning knowing. "But, that's only *if* he keeps his grades up and talks it through with you."

Pressing my lips together, I nod. I knew this was coming, and I guess I was hoping I was wrong. But I've seen the change in Colson over these past months working part-time on the ranch, and he's truly found his wings in the role. I'm not the kind of person who'll stand in his way and stop him from following his true calling.

"He really does love ranchin', doesn't he? And I *know* he's not even a kid anymore. He's a man, almost. In a few months, he'll be eighteen. It's just..."

"You didn't expect him to choose a path that would have him laid out like that as soon as you walked in after havin' a good day with the girls?"

I bob my head. "Exactly. But at the end of the day, I just want him to be happy. So, I'll be sure to sit down and have a talk with him, and make it clear that I'm not gonna be the blockade to his path."

"I reckon he'll appreciate that, angel." He lifts my hand and presses a kiss against my knuckles. "Besides, I'll be right here watchin' over him when-ever you're not around."

"There's still no excuse for my behavior back there. I really am sorry. I shouldn't have gone off the deep end like that."

"I know." His voice is so gentle that I just want to curl up against him and feel safe there forever. So I lean in close, his arm going around me as we stare out at the waterfall together.

"Do you ever worry that this was just too simple?" I ask eventually. "Like, in Aster's books about the Mountain's Call, there's always an obstacle for the couple to overcome or some kind of conflict to resolve. We haven't had any of that. We just...being together comes easy."

He arches a brow. "You think this has been easy, angel? You seem to be glossing over the part where you had me twisted up in knots for weeks before we got together, leaving me wondering if you'd ever see how good we could be together."

"Sorry... *again*."

He shakes his head. "Don't be sorry for that. Don't be sorry for anything. All of it led us to now. To you in my arms, me falling deeper in love with you every single day, and to knowin' that what-ever comes our way, we'll face it together."

Now there's no stopping my eyes from stinging with unshed tears. I dig my teeth into my quivering lip.

Beau moves an arm onto the rock behind my back and leans in, releasing my hand and gliding his fingers in my hair, moving in close. The rightness of this moment causes the last of my tension —self-inflicted at that—to ebb away.

"So you see, there's nothin' to apologize for, angel. It's all OK. Just like it's always meant to be."

'I know. I feel it in my heart. And on top of that... She told me," I whisper.

He shifts back and scrunches his nose up. "She?"

"Yeah. The Spirit. She called me to the springs. It was almost like I could *hear* her, but I know that's not possible because she's not a real person. But she's here, she's within me, within all of us. And just knowing that helped me realize a few things."

"Good things, I hope," he murmurs, wrapping an arm around me and pulling me close, his arms feeling like a warm fluffy blanket, shrouding me in his love.

I smile up at him, looking deep into his chocolate eyes I *really* hope our future children get. "You know that life hasn't been easy for us. But the kids and I are stronger for it. Losing Dad was one of the hardest things I've ever had to go through. Harder than losing Mum when I was thirteen, harder than anything." He rubs his hand up and down my back, the comfort encouraging me to keep going. "But keeping the kids together, giving up my future—at least the foreseeable one—to do that, it didn't even feel like a sacrifice to me, because providing for my brothers and sister was the *only* thing that mattered. It still is."

"I know that, Molly. And I accept it. I never want anything more from you than you can give."

"But that's the thing," I continue, knowing he's jumped to the wrong conclusion and needing to set him straight. "I want to give you *everything*. And I know I was keepin' you at arm's length for a long time. But that wasn't because of you and what we both wanted. It was because the kids and I have already had enough loss and struggles in our lives, I wasn't brave enough to take the chance on lovin' anyone else in case we lost you too."

"Fuck, angel," he says, burying his face in my neck, tightening his hug around me. "You're never gonna lose me."

"None of us can say that and mean it. Life doesn't work like that. But that also doesn't mean that I should close myself off to something wonderful because of fear." Beau lifts his head, resting his forehead against mine. "You've shown me that falling in love and opening up my heart is far better than protecting myself by keeping everyone who cares about me at bay. And I don't want to do that anymore. I want you. I want us. And I'd rather have all this happiness for a moment than live a single moment longer without it."

"You know, I thought I had a full life before I heard the Call. But it's like livin' in a world of black and white compared to the vibrant color you've brought into my life." He tilts his head and touches his lips to mine, leaving them there as his eyes bore into my tear-filled ones. "Never leavin' you, angel. You and the kids are everything to me. All I've ever wanted is to be everything back to you in return."

I frame his jaw in my hands, letting the tears fall because they're happy ones. I've never been happier in my entire life. "I know that too."

"The spirit told you that as well?"

Shaking my head, I smile. "Nope. That's something I learned from you."

Unable to hold back any longer, I kiss him, trailing my tongue along the seam of his lips before delving inside, pouring every ounce of love I have for this wonderful man—my *One*—into the connection, moaning into his mouth when he pulls me into his lap, tilts my head to the side and takes over.

"I love you, boss."

"Love you too, angel."

We kiss again but this time it's slow and sweet, it's not hot and hungry and desperate—although I have no doubt that'll come later—this is about cementing us, our future, our love for each other in a rare moment of peace and tranquility, under the never-ending watch of the Mountain Spirit. It's absolutely perfect.

"No more runnin', angel," Beau mutters roughly against my lips.

"No more runnin'."

He pulls his head back and stares straight into my eyes. "Promise?"

"I promise, Beau. If I'm gonna run anywhere, it'll be straight to you. I want everything with you. I want sons with your brown eyes and my blonde hair."

His answering grin is so bright it almost blinds me. "And I want daughters who look exactly like their mother."

"I'll see what I can do about that."

"Good," he says, kissing me quick again. "Because there's somewhere I wanna take you."

My head jerks back. "What, now?"

"Yeah. Especially if we want somewhere to put all these lookalike children we're gonna make."

'OK..." I answer slowly, wondering if maybe Beau was the one to hit his head, not my brother. "If you take me to a barn and show me a bunch of stalls, I'm gonna take everything I just said back."

"Trust me, angel," he says with a laugh. "This is one surprise you're gonna like."

"Wow. What is this place?" Molly asks as I pull the Gator up in front of my —*our*—cabin. "Did you...did you *build* this? Is this what y'all have been workin' on?"

Nodding, I cut the engine and incline my head toward the building. "Wanna see?"

We both get out and I wait for Molly to reach my side, tangling my hand with hers before I walk her up the front steps to the wraparound porch, then up to the front door, which is where we stop.

"Before we go in, I just wanna warn you that this isn't finished yet. I started building it months ago, figuring I'd have a place to call my own whenever the Call decided to send my One my way. But the Mountain Spirit moved a little quicker than I anticipated, so I've been workin' out here with my brothers and Miller whenever the chance arose."

"So, this is your cabin?"

I nod. "Yeah. But when you're ready, I'd like for it to be ours someday."

"The kids too?"

Reaching up, I brush a strand of flyaway blonde hair behind her ear and press a lingering kiss against her temple. "Most definitely. I want them to be my family too."

Closing her eyes for a moment, she takes a deep breath and smiles. "Family. Yes, Beau. That's all I want."

"Then let me show you the space my brothers and I created for this family of ours," I say, pushing the front door open and letting her step through first.

After getting the drywall up, we went to work on the kitchen and the bathrooms, and now all that's left is to put in the electrics, finish the floors, and paint. I give it another month tops, but even without all those things, the place still looks great. It looks like it's meant to be a home.

"I can't believe you did all this," she says, moving in further and running her hand over the mantle above the hearth, her eyes going up to the exposed beam ceilings and over to the kitchen with countertops made from lumber we sourced from the ranch itself.

"Does that mean you like it?" I slide my hands in the back pockets of my jeans, rocking on my toes as I watch closely for her reaction. So far, I'm seeing awe and surprise. But I want to be sure there's some joy in there too.

"Like it?" She turns and meets my eyes before she swallows down hard and smiles. "Beau, I love it. I can't believe you spent all your free time building me a home." She walks around the cabin and notes the many rooms surrounding the living space. "A home that's big enough for my siblings too, and for all those babies we're gonna make." She places a hand over her mouth and releases a shuddered breath, tears pooling in her eyes. "It's amazin'. I never dreamed...never expected...never *hoped.*"

Moving over to her, I slide my arms around her waist and tuck my face against the curve of her neck, pressing soft kisses against the delicate skin. "Dream away, angel," I whisper. "Hope for everything this life can ever give you, and I'll find a way to make it yours. From this moment forth, I am yours to command."

With a tear-filled laugh, she turns in my arms and places a hand against my cheek, bringing her lips to mine and kissing me soft and slow before wrapping her arms around my neck and just holding herself to me. "Thank you. Thank you for everything you've done, everything you're going to do, and for just being you."

She tightens her hold and I do the same, hugging her a little tighter. Because it doesn't escape me that this is the first time she's accepted something from me without mentioning a repayment of some kind. Just that alone feels like I'm winning. But there's still one thing that will make this day, this union, feel utterly complete.

"You're more than welcome, angel," I say, pulling back slightly and taking both of her hands in mine. "And normally, I'd never ask anything of you. But there is one thing I'd really like for you to do for me. If you're willin'."

She nods rapidly. "Anything, Beau. Just ask and I'll say yes. You've turned my life into a happily ever after from a great romance novel. So there's nothing I wouldn't do to thank you for that."

"I was hopin' you'd say somethin' to that effect," I say with a smirk as I lower to the ground and take one knee.

"Wha-what are you doing?" Her eyes bug out as I release one of her hands so I can fish around in my pocket for the ring that's been waiting for a moment just like this. "Beau?"

When my fingers connect with the metal band, I pull the solitaire diamond ring from my pocket and hold it up to my One. "I'm askin' you to marry me, Molly. Will you do me the honor of becomin' my wife?"

"Yes. Yes. Yes. Yes. Yes," she repeats, nodding emphatically as she bounces on her toes while I try to get the ring attached to her wriggling body.

"Hold still, will ya?"

She forces herself steady as nervous laughter bubbles out of her. "I'm sorry. I just never thought...I never..."

"Dreamed," I finish for her as I get the ring settled at the base of her finger. "I know, angel. But now you can. Dream as big and as crazy as you want."

With a quick glance at the ring on her finger, she flings herself at me and wraps her arms around my neck, our faces almost colliding before she pauses, right before our lips touch. "This, right here," she whispers. "This is my dream. You, me, the kids, and a happy future. It's all I want."

"Then it's yours," I whisper back, bringing her mouth to mine and kissing her deeper and hungrier than before, knowing deep inside, right down to my soul that this is it, the completion of the Call. Molly and I have surrendered to it and to each other, and nothing has ever felt sweeter.

"Wait," Molly says, pulling her head back just as things start to get heated.

"What's wrong?"

"Do I get to choose the colors of this place?"

I can't help but laugh as I wrap her up tight and carry her over to the kitchen counter. "Of course."

"What if I want hot pink walls in the living area?"

"Then we'll have a hot pink living area," I say with a chuckle.

"And what if I want glow-in-the-dark penises painted all over our bedroom ceiling?"

"As long as it's *my* dick you're painting up there, go for it."

She pulls back a little and looks into my eyes, hers filled with nothing but delight. "I don't want any of those things, but I love that you'd give them to me if I did want them. You have the most beautiful heart, Beau Barnes. And I'm going to spend the rest of my life making sure you never doubt for a second how much I'm in love with you."

"Ditto, Molly Roberts. Ditto," I say, bringing my mouth back to hers before peeling off some of her layers and having my first and most favorite meal in the kitchen of our new home.

## MOLLY

"I need some more packing tape," Sage calls out from her open bedroom door.

"I've got some," Colson replies.

"Is this us testing out the acoustics of a nearly empty house or do we just like yelling at each other?" I ask, joining in on the 'shout at each other across the hallway party' we're having.

We're finishing off the last of our packing because today we're officially moving out of our childhood family home and into the cabin Beau built—with the help of his brothers and the kids. It's kind of surreal. At first, I was sad about leaving this house behind, but since it's freehold and has so many memories from over the years attached to it, Beau suggested, and the kids and I agreed, that we didn't need to sell it. So that's why it's now going to be rented out. The bonus is that the extra income will help boost the kid's college funds—well those going to college, anyway, since Colson and I finally sat down and had a good talk about his own personal 'call' to the land—and it'll also mean I can work less and have more time for me, Beau, and the kids.

So, although this is a goodbye to living here, the property will still be staying in the family. Something that made the decision to move to the ranch a hell of a lot easier, let me tell you.

"Angel," Beau muses, appearing in my bedroom doorway, leaning a sexy shoulder against the frame. *Yes, I'm that girl.* I find even the smallest, most obscure things on my fiance's body arousing. Like the way his brows knit tightly together when he's thinking real hard about something. Or the just how his shoulder muscles tense and release when he whips his shirt off to move hay bales, or stock... or when he's hovering over me, driving his body into mine while my hands grip him tight and he—

Beau's chuckle snaps me out of my lustful daze, his eyes dancing with amusement and hooded interest as he rakes his gaze over my body. "Whatever you're thinkin', angel, remember it for tonight, cause that look on your face tells me I'm *really* gonna like whatever it is."

"What if I'm thinkin' about you doin' the dishes?"

He shrugs. "Wouldn't be the first time."

"Or foldin' the laundry?" A small grin plays on my lips.

"Will those lacey panties I like be in there?"

I stand up from my perch on the bed and cross the room, wrapping my arms around his waist, smiling up at him, and dropping my voice to a low, sultry whisper.

"Probably not. I'm wearin' them right now." His hands go to my waist and he grunts. "Oh, I know what I was thinkin' about. How sexy you'll look while vacuumin'."

Beau rolls his hips against mine in a silent sexy promise as he dips his mouth down to touch my lips. "Whatever you want, angel. Might even do it naked if the house is empty."

I shudder, suddenly wishing the house was empty right now. Doesn't matter how much time we spend together, how much time we're apart, there could be a million people mulling around us and I'd still sense Beau, still feel his heart beating in sync with mine. It's unreal how close we are now, and that's about to get a whole lot more now that we're all moving into the cabin. Beau and I slept there last night, having our first night together alone in our new home while the kids, Jesse, and Kendra slept here at the old house having a packing party with music, junk food, and a whole lot of fun—Cody's description, not mine.

"You sure need more boxes, angel? Because I swear I need another six months to extend the cabin if we're gonna fit all of this stuff in there." His warm expression makes me melt inside. This doesn't bode well for me in future arguments. Then again, if the makeup sex we had after my freakout when Colson hurt himself is anything to go by, maybe a little playful fight now and then wouldn't be so bad...

"I'll have you know that most of this stuff is going into storage. It's not that much, boss. I promise."

"Hey," he murmurs, lifting his knuckles and gently rubbing them over my cheek. "I was only teasing. You can bring absolutely anythin' and everythin' you wanna bring to *our* cabin. Because it's gonna be *our* home, not just mine. *Ours*. And I can't wait to walk in after a long, hard day workin' the land to a house full of *our* stuff."

"Thank you," I whisper.

He lifts his head, his forehead bunching a little. *Damn, even that is a bit sexy.* "You don't have to thank me for anythin', angel. This is just the be-ginnin' of what's gonna be a beautiful life to-gether. I know you've got a lot of memories in this house, but I'm lookin' forward to makin' a whole lot more of our own too."

"I want that too."

He presses his lips to mine, holding them there for a moment while we just breathe each other in. Then he touches the tip of his tongue to mine and I melt into him, running my hands up his back and holding him close as he slowly, thoroughly claims every inch of my mouth.

It's only when we hear the sound of a truck door slamming shut from the driveway that we pull apart. Beau gives me a parting peck on the lips before telling me he'll go see who it is. I step out and watch him walk away because it doesn't matter how many times I see it, I'll never tire of staring at that man.

Cols pokes his head out his bedroom door, catching my eye. "Hey, Molls. You're drooling again." He winks at me, but his smile is soft, and I know he's happy for me, for all of us. Because after years of working hard and struggling, we're still standing, and somehow life and Beau—with a little help from the Mountain Spirit—have shown me that I can provide for my family and be everything they need me to be while not having to sacrifice my own happiness to do that.

I shoot Colson a smirk. "Just you wait, brother. One day you're gonna meet your one and only, and you'll wanna check out her butt when she leaves a room too. Not for a while though, OK?"

He rolls his eyes. "Whatever you say, Molls."

It's then all packing is momentarily forgotten about because the cavalry arrives.

"Let's get this party started," Sawyer announces, filling the front doorway with his tall brawny body. He's even still wearing his cowboy hat on his head so he barely clears the top of the frame as he walks in and surveys the half-empty house filled with stacked boxes before flexing for show. "Heard you needed some muscle."

"You heard correctly. But I thought maybe you'd bring a little more muscle with you."

His brow shoots up. "You think I can't carry this all on my own?"

"Thinking and knowing are two different things."

"Maybe I oughta turn right back around and head home," he says, the smirk curling his lips telling me he doesn't mean a word.

"You know, if I didn't know better, I'd say you almost didn't *want* to help us move," I tease, just as Randy, Miller, Jesse, and a few of the Barnes' cousins pile into the room.

Sawyer gasps and places a hand on his chest. "Aww, Molls. I'm shocked you'd think that about me. I'm always happy to help. Especially if it means my brother is smilin' all the time."

"You just want the bunkhouse to yourself," Miller says, nudging Sawyer with his shoulder. "There'll probably be more knockin' boots than bunking down."

"Well, that ain't gonna happen cause Cols is moving into one of the other rooms to keep me company. It'll be bachelor town in there again."

"Bachelor town?" I repeat, giving him a stern look.

"Don't worry, Molls, I'm gonna be on my *best* behavior."

"Maybe that's what I'm worried about," I say with a laugh, trying to hide my real thoughts on the subject since Colson is a month off eighteen now and was rather insistent that we let him move straight into the bunkhouse rather than into the cabin with all of us. It took a bit of convincing, but when Randy assured me he'd keep a close eye on him, coupled with the fact our cabin is literally moments away, I relented. Especially since he'll be working all of his spare hours around school and sport on the ranch now that breeding season is coming up. Even though I'm sad that he doesn't want to go to college, I'm proud that he seems so sure of what he wants to do in life. But just to be sure, this will be the perfect time to throw him in the deep end and make sure he's one hundred percent committed to the rancher life before anything about his senior year is final.

I'm not sure Sawyer, with his perpetual bachelordom and determination that the call is not and *will* not happen to him, quite gel well with my aspirations for the man I hope Colson will become. But I remind myself that he'll also be working side by side with Beau, Miller, Jesse, and Randy. And at least *they* have their head screwed on properly, giving Colson some fine male role models to aspire to be like Cody too, for that matter.

Then again, we can't give up on Sawyer just yet. Kendra has been having a lot of dreams lately, and although she's been very tight-lipped about what they're about, or more importantly, *who* they're about, we've got a betting pool going over who we think it might be. Right now, most of us are picking Sawyer as the next one to hear the Call. But Kendra—to her credit—*hasn't* put in a wager. But Jesse has. And something tells me there's a little bit of insider knowledge being shared in their marital bed, because he sure as hell put down a lot of money on Sawyer getting knocked on his butt by a girl by the end of the Summer. That's the Seer way though, tip and tease and never quite tell us everything. I guess we'll get used to it in the end.

"All right," Beau calls out to everyone. "Let's get this truck loaded and move on out!"

A few hours later, with everyone chipping in to help with the heavy lifting—except Kendra because she announced that she and Jesse are expecting a baby, which is super exciting. Miller teased her that she timed it that way on purpose to get out of helping us move. But that just earned him an elbow to the ribs from Ellie-Mae, who *also* had a little announcement of her own. Another baby is coming to Eagle Mountain Ranch!

I thought breeding season was just for the cows, but if two out of three women are currently pregnant on the ranch, I'm drinking nothing but bottled water since there's obviously *something* in the water here.

Although Beau and I *want* children, we also still have Sage and Cody at home, and I want time with Beau and them first before bringing babies into the mix. But not too much time, of course.

With the packing done, and all the boxes now in trucks being driven to the ranch, it leaves just Beau, me, Colson, Sage, and Cody standing in the now-empty house. And boy, are the emotions hitting me hard.

Beau wraps his arms around my waist from behind, pressing his chest to my back and brushing his lips against my neck. "I'll wait for you guys in the car."

I turn in his arms, my eyes searching his. "You don't have to."

"Yeah, angel. You four take your moment to say goodbye, and I'll be ready to drive you home when you're ready."

"Home," I repeat with a happy sigh.

"Our home," he says.

"I love you, you know that?"

"To the end of days, angel." He kisses me softly. "I love you too."

Then he cups Colson's shoulder, hugs Sage, and ruffles Cody's hair before disappearing outside.

"I thought I'd be sadder," Sage says. "But I'm not. This just feels like another step forward, you know?"

I nod. "We had a lot of good times here though, right?"

"And some shit ones," Colson adds, and I don't even bother calling him out for cursing.

"But the cabin's gonna be cool. And we can still come here and visit. Right, Molls?" Cody asks. I wrap my arm around his shoulder and pull him into my side. "Absolutely. This is still and will always be ours, we're just gonna be makin' a new home with Beau on the ranch."

"I can't *wait* to get a pet pig," Cody announces, bouncing on his feet.

All three of us jerk our gazes his way. "Say what now?" Sage blurts out, giving voice to what the rest of us are probably thinking.

"A pet pig. Like the one from that movie that talks. I want one of those. Then I can teach Spencer to ride *that* since he didn't wanna ride Gertie."

*Oh lord help me.* One thing's for sure, ranch life will never be boring with Cody around.

Then again, it's like Beau said when we were up at Paradise. I'd much rather live in a world of vibrant color than one in black and white.

And with Beau, Kendra, and all the rest of the Barnes family members in our lives now, something tells me there'll never be a dull day again. Especially when a certain bull rider hears the Call....

# EPILOGUE 1

BEAU

*Five years later...*

"Come on, angel. You're doin' great," I say, nursing a snuffling bundle in my arms as my wife clutches my sleeve and gives one last almighty push, delivering the second of our twin boys, Bryant and Briggs, like the champ she is. "I'm so proud of you."

"Oh god, I never wanna go through that again," she pants, crying and smiling all at the same time as Briggs is placed on her belly, and I place Bryant next to him, too. "I can't believe we've got twin boys, Beau. Just look at their little faces."

"Gorgeous like their mom," I say, pressing a kiss to the top of her sweaty head.

"I was gonna say handsome like their dad. But if you insist." She turns her head to smile at me, and I capture her upturned mouth in a kiss, breathing her in as my heart swells with pride and joy and gratitude at the most amazing gift anyone could have given me—a family.

There have been many times in our relationship where Molly would insist that she had to *do* something for me to show her gratitude. And each time, I honestly couldn't think of a single thing I wanted besides her happiness as a reward. But seeing these two beautiful bundles rooting around on her chest for their first meal has me realizing that this right here is the greatest gift of all, it's more repayment than money or time or favors. Because now I get these little guys for a lifetime. I get to raise them and watch them grow with her. The mountain has truly blessed us all.

"Thank you, angel," I say, touching the twins lightly on their downy little heads. "Thank you for givin' me not one, but two children. I'm so fuc—"

"Beau!" Molly admonishes with a half-hearted laugh. "Watch your language 'round the little'uns. They're impressionable, you know."

Biting my mouth closed, I chuckle slightly and correct my faux pas. "What I was tryna say is that you've made me so *incredibly* happy, angel."

"Me too, boss. I honestly don't think I could be happier."

Giving her a kiss again, we take a moment just admiring our babies while the midwives clean up the room before giving me a crash course on how to change and dress a newborn while Molly takes a shower and we prepare to move her onto the maternity ward with the other new moms.

By the time we're wheeled over there, most of the family is already waiting. And a few at a time, they all come in and meet the new additions. Although, Colson gets a little too caught up chatting to the midwife, possibly trying out some of Sawyer's tried-and-true moves on the pretty little nurse. She's blushing plenty, so I guess he's got a knack for romancing the ladies. Sawyer will be proud.

"Oh gosh, I can't believe I'm an aunty," Sage squeals, clasping her hands at her chest when she takes in the sight of the two bundled babes. "They're sooooo adorable. Can I take them back to college with me in my luggage?" Sage has taken a week away from her psychology studies to be here to welcome her nephews into the world. She flashes Molly a cheeky smile and Molly chuckles.

"Not on your life. Do you have any idea how hard it was to grow then birth these two? I'm keepin' them close until they're at least thirty."

Sage laughs while sixteen-year-old Cody scrunches up his face. "Wouldn't they get hurt bein' in a suitcase?"

"She's jokin' you numbnut," Colson says, tapping his brother lightly on the back of the head. "Those teenage hormones of yours aren't doin' your brain any favors."

"Hey!" Cody replies with a scowl.

"Don't worry about it, kid," I say, reaching out and giving his arm a squeeze. "It happens to us all."

"So what are their names? And do I get to be called Uncle Cody?"

"Bryant and Briggs," Molly says with a serene smile. "And if you want to be Uncle Cody, that's what you'll be."

"I wanna just be called 'Unc'," Colson says, nodding as he folds his muscular arms across his chest. Hard work on the ranch has seen him filling out a lot these past few years.

"Unc, huh?" Molly says with a nod. "Very manly."

"Too right," Colson adds. "I'm gonna teach them all about ranchin', just like how Beau and his brothers taught me."

"I'm gonna teach them how to choose the right rope to make a lasso," Cody adds.

"And I'm gonna teach them to be emotionally stable and well-rounded individuals who are in touch with their feelings," our budding psychologist, Sage, says as she presses a light finger touch to Brigg's chin. "Gosh, they're just so dang cute!"

"Yeah," Molly says around a yawn. "Beau and I make pretty babies, that's for sure."

"How about you guys head on home and let Molly get some rest?" I suggest.

"I'm OK," Molly says, yawning again.

"Yeah, right." Colson laughs. "Beau's right. You should definitely rest. We'll come see you tomorrow. Ellie-Mae said she's cookin' a big feast up at the ranch house to celebrate the twins' arrival, and that generally means some yummy desserts. So I'll save you both some and bring it in, yeah?"

"That'd be amazin'," I say, rising to my feet to walk them all out because we opted for a family room where I get to stay the night with Molly as well. And it's a good thing too, there's no way I'm spending a night without my One. The idea of it feels like torture.

"And then there were four," Molly says, when I return to the seat by her side. "Can you believe we're parents now?"

"Yeah, I can," I say, kissing her on the forehead as I brush her freshly washed hair from her head. "And we're gonna be great at it. These boys are gonna feel so loved."

"Oh, I know. You have such an incredible capacity to love. They'll never miss out on a thing with you as their daddy."

"And they'll be so well cared for and know so much joy and patience with you as their momma. But to do that, angel, you're gonna need some rest."

Her eyes blink slowly closed. "Why are you still always tellin' me to rest?"

"Because if I don't, you'll never stop."

She grins. "You know me too well."

"I love you with everything I have."

"Yeah. You do. And I love you too, boss."

Her sleepy words make me smile as she drifts off, and I turn my attention to our tiny, sleeping sons. And as I sit there in the quiet of the hospital room surrounded by my greatest loves, I realize that this is it. This is the epitome of happiness. And all it took to get here was a little patience, and a fated Call from a Mountain Spirit. Something I hope continues on throughout the family for generation after generation.

## EPILOGUE 2

MOLLY

*Ten years later...*

One can say that after more than ten years of being together, you have to occasionally spice things up in the bedroom, and today is no different. With three kids, a successful ever-expanding ranch to run, and me working at both the Vet Clinic and Horse Haven, my husband and I make the most of any time alone we can steal together. And when it comes with an empty house like today... Well, let's just say my husband is in for one heck of a surprise when he comes home.

I sent him a text twenty minutes ago, asking if he'd like to come home for lunch. And the sound of galloping horse hooves getting closer to the house means it's almost go time.

I'm trembling with anticipation as I lean into the bedroom doorway off the side of the living room, posing seductively in my black cowboy boots, Beau's favorite black Stetson, and nothing else. The butterflies in my tummy and the tingles coursing *everywhere* have me barely able to breathe, let alone stop myself from panting.

The cabin is dead quiet, with our five-year-old twins, Bryant and Briggs, and our little three-year-old girl, Bethany, currently having a playdate with their cousins at Ellie-Mae and Miller's house. And that's all the cabin houses these days since Cody is away at college finishing up his senior year in marine biology—having decided his love of water *and* animals was where his passion lied—but still lives here when he comes home, and Sage now lives in the old house we grew up in, working as a counselor and child psychologist, helping kids and families from all around the district. And of course, Colson is still in the bunkhouse, living his best life.

Sucking my breath in when I hear Beau's boots hit the porch, I do one last reposition to make sure I look as sultry as possible. Then his hand turns the doorknob, my heart pounding as I hold my position and wait for Beau's beautiful brown eyes to lift to mine.

The moment they do, it's like the entire world stands still around us and the only thing in focus, the only thing I can see is my husband's smile morph from happy to absolutely ravenous as he stills for barely a second before launching himself across the room and near on tackling me. His arms separate, his fingers of one hand dragging into my hair, the other wrapping around my hip and gripping my ass as he slams his mouth down on mine with a guttural growl I feel down to my bones. Then he pushes his hard-as-steel, denim-covered cock against my bare mound.

I squeak with surprise against his tongue when I'm suddenly lifted in the air and carried across the room, the hat falling onto the ground and my boots kicked away as my back hits the mattress and I'm left staring up to watch Beau toe off his boots and near on rip all his clothes off until he's deliciously naked and oh so hard in front of me.

Putting a knee to the bed, he prowls over my body, dragging his lips over every inch of skin he passes, swiping his pointed tongue through my soaked seam and circling my swollen clit before moving his mouth over my stomach and nuzzling my breasts until his lips are hovering over mine and his hard everywhere body is pushing mine into the bed.

"Would've gotten here a fuck of a lot faster had I known *this* was how you were waitin' for me, angel."

I run my fingers through his unruly hat hair and smirk up at him. "Where's the fun in that, boss?"

He growls low and deep, and all kinds of rumbly before taking my mouth again, thrusting his tongue into my mouth and claiming my lips with renewed vigor as I cling to him, running my hands over his shoulders and back as I hook my ankles behind his thighs and roll my hips up against his, whimpering every time the head of his cock slides over my clit.

"Need you, Beau," I moan in his ear, spreading my legs wide just as he notches himself at my entrance and braces himself above me, his hungry eyes locked with mine as he jerks his hips and slams his way home.

He pulls back then slams them deep back inside me, over and over again, as deep and as hard as he can go, his rock-solid length. Barreling into my slick heat over and over again

"Fuck. So fucking tight around me." His voice comes out rough and raspy as he meshes his lips with mine and swallows my whimpers and moans. Our body's move as one, pushing each other higher and higher, the sounds of our love-making filling the air as we let ourselves go, his cock pounding in and out of me, driving me higher, sending me soaring,

He nips and sucks the skin of my neck, as he braces himself on one arm, reaching between us and strumming his fingers over my clit in time with his strokes inside of me, increasing the pressure and raking his teeth against my skin. My cries get louder, my moans longer, and my limbs tighter around him, holding on for dear life as my climax takes hold.

My entire body goes rigid, my back arching and my hips bucking wildly as I scream his name so loud it probably echoes across the fields "Beau. Yes. Oh, God."

I don't even have time to come down from my high before another wave of pleasure washes over me I can't help but watch Beau lose his own battle, gritting his teeth and thrusting deep, planting himself as far as he can go and growling out his release as he digs his teeth into my skin.

"Fuck, angel. Never gonna forget the sight of you waiting for me in my hat and nothing else."

"Good," I murmur, totally sated and spent and unable to move, let alone wipe the grin off my face.

Beau lifts his head and smiles down at me. "Gonna have to make lunch at home a regular thing. A whole lot better than eatin' sandwiches in the fields and looking at cattle."

"Maybe next time you can come home to *me* wearing nothing but a hat."

He chuckles and brushes his lips against mine, his eyes twinkling with mischief as he pushes up off the bed, walking over to the corner of the room and bending over—giving me a mighty good view of his backside—before turning around and standing there, naked as the day he was born, wearing nothing but his hat and a sexy smirk.

"To your satisfaction, Mrs. Barnes?" he croons.

I squirm against the mattress, my body *definitely* on board for another round before Beau has to go back to work again. "Saddle up, cowboy. Mama's in the mood for another ride."

"Fuck, angel. I love you."

"I know. And if you come over here, I'll show you just how much I love you in that hat."

...wait! How about a FREE mountain man book to tide you over?
Tap this image or click the link below

Free book link: (newsletter opt in required)
https://dl.bookfunnel.com/h6c7b5gbl1

Annnnnd don't go away yet. Beau's story is next in Cowboy Seeks a Healer. Tap the image and grab it here—>

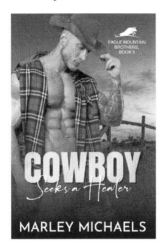

Sign up for my newsletter to receive release day emails: https://www.subscribepage.com/marleymichaels

Don't forget to add marleymichaelswrites@gmail.com to your address book!

If you're on social media, you can catch me on Facebook

https://www.facebook.com/authormarleymichaels/

or join my reader group

www.facebook.com/groups/856031968231022

Or you can follow me on Instagram

https://instagram.com/marleymichaelswrites

Can't wait to have more fun on the Mountains with you!

# MARLEY MICHAELS READING ORDER

## Moose Mountain Brothers

Author Seeking Mountain Man

Introvert Seeking Mountain Man

Fangirl Seeking Mountain Man

Hiker Seeking Mountain Man

## Men of Moose Mountain

Mountain Seeking Doctor

Mountain Seeking Pilot

Mountain Seeking Hero

Mountain Seeking Fire Chief

Mountain Seeking Veterinarian

Mountain Seeking Princess

Mountain Seeking Santa

## Bear Mountain Brothers

Wallflower Seeks Mountain Man

Reporter Seeks Mountain Man

Artist Seeks Mountain Man

Baker Seeks Mountain Man

Dancer Seeks Mountain Man

Teacher Seeks Mountain Man

Runaway Seeks Mountain Man

Little Dove Seeks Mountain Man

Cowgirl Seeks Mountain Man

**Eagle Mountain Brothers**

Cowboy Seeks a Horse Whisperer

Cowboy Seeks a Romantic

Cowboy Seeks a Healer

Printed in Great Britain
by Amazon